CHERRY AMES NURSE STORIES

CHERRY AMES
PRIVATE DUTY NURSE

By

HELEN WELLS

SPRINGER PUBLISHING COMPANY
New York

Copyright © 1946 by Grosset & Dunlap, Inc.
Copyright © renewed 2007 by Harriet Schulman Forman
Springer Publishing Company, LLC

All rights reserved.

No part of this publication may be reproduced, stored in a retrieval system, or transmitted in any form or by any means, electronic, mechanical, photocopying, recording, or otherwise, without the prior permission of Springer Publishing Company, LLC.

Springer Publishing Company, LLC
11 West 42nd Street, 15th Floor
New York, NY 10036-8002

Acquisitions Editor: Sally J. Barhydt
Production Editor: Matthew Byrd
Cover design by Takeout Graphics, Inc.
Composition: Techbooks

08 09 10/5 4 3 2

Library of Congress Cataloging-in-Publication Data

Wells, Helen, 1910–
  Cherry Ames, private duty nurse / by Helen Wells.
    p. cm.— (Cherry Ames nurse stories)
  Summary: Cherry is finally discharged from the Army and takes a job as a private duty nurse to a celebrated musician suffering from a heart condition.
  ISBN 0-8261-0398-7 (alk. paper)
  [1. Nurses—Fiction. 2. Musicians—Fiction.] I. Title.

PZ7.W4644Cf 2006
[Fic]—dc22

2006022323

Printed in the United States of America by Bang Printing

Contents

	Foreword	iv
I	Strange Beginning	1
II	R.F.D.	20
III	Do, Re, Mi and Company	41
IV	The Fortunetellers	64
V	On Tour	84
VI	Reunion	96
VII	Romance in Reverse	117
VIII	The Threat	129
IX	Night Vigil	143
X	A Wig, A Lure, A Lie	156
XI	Nocturnal Visitor	170
XII	Miss Ames Is "Detained"	180
XIII	Trapped!	205
XIV	Troubles and Triumphs	213

Foreword

~~~~~~

Helen Wells, the author of the Cherry Ames stories, said, "I've always thought of nursing, and perhaps you have, too, as just about the most exciting, important, and rewarding, profession there is. Can you think of any other skill that is *always* needed by everybody, everywhere?"

I was and still am a fan of Cherry Ames. Her courageous dedication to her patients; her exciting escapades; her thirst for knowledge; her intelligent application of her nursing skills; and the respect she achieved as a registered nurse (RN) all made it clear to me I was going to follow in her footsteps and become a nurse—nothing else would do. Thousands of other young people were motivated by Cherry Ames to become RNs as well. Cherry Ames motivated young people on into the 1970s, when the series ended. Readers who remember reading these books in the past will enjoy rereading them now—whether or not

FOREWORD v

they chose nursing as a career—and perhaps sharing them with others.

My career has been a rich and satisfying one, during which I have delivered babies, saved lives, and cared for people in hospitals and in their homes. I have worked at the bedside and served as an administrator. I have published journals, written articles, taught students, consulted, and given expert testimony. Never once did I regret my decision to enter nursing.

During the time that I was publishing a nursing journal, I became acquainted with Robert Wells, brother of Helen Wells. In the course of conversation I learned that Ms. Wells had passed on and left the Cherry Ames copyright to Mr. Wells. Because there is a shortage of nurses here in the US today, I thought, "Why not bring Cherry back to motivate a whole new generation of young people? Why not ask Mr. Wells for the copyright to Cherry Ames?" Mr. Wells agreed, and the republished series is dedicated both to Helen Wells, the original author, and to her brother, Robert Wells, who transferred the rights to me. I am proud to ensure the continuation of Cherry Ames into the twenty-first century.

The final dedication is to you, both new and old readers of Cherry Ames: It is my dream that you enjoy Cherry's nursing skills as well as her escapades. I hope that young readers will feel motivated to choose nursing as their life's work. Remember, as Helen Wells herself said: there's no other skill that's *"always* needed by everybody, everywhere."

Harriet Schulman Forman, RN, EdD
Series Editor

CHAPTER I

Strange Beginning

CHERRY GAVE THE PILLOW A POKE AND SLEEPILY SAT UP. She shook her short, black curls off her red cheeks, and wriggled to the edge of the bed to see out the window. She was in the one place where a lively young nurse never expected to be—home! She was right here in her own room, in her own house, in her own small town of Hilton, Illinois. Her merry red-and-white room with its sun-filled windows was a highly satisfactory place to be, this sweet-smelling June morning, especially after traipsing with the Army Nurse Corps from the Pacific across the Atlantic, with flights in between, and then being a veterans' nurse besides.

"Yes *sir,* for once I stay put!" Cherry thought. "No more Army nursing. No more flight nursing. No more veterans' nursing. In fact, gosh darn it, no more nursing! Ames is just going to *sit.* For at least three months."

She lay back, luxuriously turning over in her mind all the lazy, spendthrift ways to fill her hard-earned rest period. She could play tennis today. Or go to the movies—even go to two movies, one right after the other, pausing only for a chocolate sundae in between. She could lie in the garden hammock beside her mother's fragrant flower beds, and read or simply daydream and nap. That was what Dr. Joe had ordered, after her arduous Army years. Or she could go for a swim—or some of her mother's friends had been laughing about driving over to the next town to attend a séance—or she and her young friend Midge could go to the music shop and listen to all the new swing records, and maybe buy two—

"Yes, I'm free now to do any of those things," Cherry thought restlessly, winding and unwinding one black curl around her finger. "But I don't want to very much. Guess I'm still so wound up from Army excitement that I can't relax yet." Cherry sat up again and stretched. Then she shook her dark, curly head. "Doggone, why am I bursting with energy and rarin' to go—just when I'm supposed to rest? Who wants to do nothing, anyhow? Rarin' to go—but go *where*?"

The little white clock ticking away on her dressing table said eight o'clock—shamefully early. Cherry deliberately dawdled her way through bathing and dressing. She finally chose her red sports dress to put on. It flamed no less than her cherry-red cheeks and lips, and set off her brilliant dark eyes and hair. Sports sandals.

No stockings. One bracelet, for fun. Cherry stood straight and slim and graceful before her mirror, a vivid and strikingly pretty girl. But her thoughts skipped happily past her good looks and on to breakfast. As usual, at any hour of the day or night, Cherry was hungry.

She went out into the upstairs hall and peeked at her parents' door, to see if they were up. The door was closed. Charlie's door stood open, onto her brother's unoccupied room. Her twin brother was still with the Army of Occupation in Japan. Cherry looked in at his airplane models, the neat, empty bed, the masculine pennants and photographs and technical books. Her own snapshot, she saw, still had the place of honor on his dresser.

Cherry sighed, and tiptoed along the hall. As she passed her parents' big room, she heard her father whistling merrily, if slightly off key, behind the closed door. But from downstairs floated the aroma of coffee and oranges. Her mother must be up. Cherry sniffed hopefully, and started down the long, broad, winding stairs of their Victorian house.

She descended as far as the first landing, with its high window of green and rose and blue and amber panes, when an impulse seized her. Looking cautiously around, she saw no one in sight. Happily, she climbed onto the banister, gripped with hands and knees, and let go. Whee! She flew down the banister at glorious speed, abruptly stopping at the bottom with a thump.

"Shocking behavior for a graduate nurse!"

It was her mother, pausing in the doorway with a tray of breakfast things, laughing at her.

Cherry unscrambled herself from the banister and ran over to kiss her pretty dark-eyed mother.

"I do a high, wide, and handsome slide, you'll have to admit that," Cherry boasted.

"You had a better technique when you were seven."

"But Charlie was the champion." Cherry filched a piece of toast from the tray, and munched. She followed her mother into the spacious dining room. "He went down no-hands. Ah, youth! Any chores today, lady?"

"No chores for you, honey. You rest. Just sit down now and drink this orange juice." Her mother vanished into the kitchen.

"How you bully me into resting!" Cherry called after her. She picked up her glass of orange juice and, sipping, wandered around the sunny bay window, inspecting the waxy green plants which thrived there.

"How your mother bullies me, too," said Mr. Ames, coming in with the morning newspaper. His humorous face looked fresh and rested this summer morning. His light hair, even with its gray, his tall solid figure, looked so much like Charlie's that Cherry swallowed hard with lonesomeness. It was not much fun being free to play, while her twin still served overseas.

"But today," Mr. Ames said loudly, toward the kitchen, "is my day to bully your mother for a change."

STRANGE BEGINNING

He sat down at the table, and he and Cherry exchanged grins.

Edith Ames came back carrying a hot platter of bacon and eggs. "Who bullies whom, and why?"

Mr. Ames put down his newspaper. "Are you really going to that tomfool séance with the rest of those silly women?"

"Oh, why not? It will be fun. Perfectly harmless."

"I don't believe fortunetelling is ever harmless. And to bother driving over to the next town for such nonsense—Well, suit yourself. I see you won't be bullied." Mr. Ames added with a chuckle, "But don't let 'em tell you they see a tall, dark, moneyed stranger coming into your life, understand?"

Mrs. Ames grinned deliciously. "Why, Will, I thought *you* were the man in my life. Or aren't you?"

"Better be," Mr. Ames said gruffly and buried his face in the newspaper. Mrs. Ames poured coffee and smiled to herself. Cherry noticed with quiet pleasure that her parents were still very much in love with each other.

"Cherry, perhaps you'd like to come along to the séance—her mother offered.

"I don't feel particularly ghostly today," Cherry said. "But if I can't think of anything better to do—I've got to find something, I can't just sit on my thumbs—"

Her father said, "Your old friend, Dr. Fortune, has an idea for you."

"Dr. Joe?"

"Mm-hmm. Met him downtown on his way to the clinic yesterday. He believes you should rest, of course. But he knows you're too restless to do absolutely nothing. Said he'd thought up a 'light activity' for you."

Cherry was interested at once. "What was it?"

"He didn't say, sweetie. Maybe"—Mr. Ames glanced slyly at his wife—"maybe the fortuneteller will say."

"I'll tell you what my father said!" shrilled a voice from the open bay windows. "Isn't it strange how I always go calling at mealtime?"

It was Midge Fortune, Dr. Joe's teen-age, motherless daughter. Her light-brown hair and gray-green hazel eyes showed just above the window boxes.

"Can we invite you to breakfast?" Mrs. Ames called. "And don't climb in over the plants!"

"Yes, Mrs. Ames! Thank you!" Midge's head disappeared and in twenty seconds, she had banged through the front door, through the living room, and landed at the dining table with a fork in her hand.

"My dad said he could get you a chance at—"

"Good morning, Midge," Mr. Ames said, mock-severely.

"Good morning. My father thought Cherry'd—"

"A fine day, Miss Fortune," Cherry chanted.

"A scrumptious day, Miss Ames. Dad said you ought to have a try at—"

"Bacon and eggs, Midgie?" Mrs. Ames asked. "Or are you trying to diet again?"

STRANGE BEGINNING

"Ladies and gentlemen, I mean sir," the teen-ager said earnestly, "you know perfectly well I would eat nails, and good morning to you all including any stray dogs and cats, and will you *please* let me tell you Dad's idea for Cherry, because it is a humdinger?"

Cherry turned her brilliant dark gaze on her and said bewilderingly, "How would you like to go to a séance—

"A what? What do you wear?"

Mr. Ames rose from the table in good-humored disgust. "I'm going downtown now. Down where there are some sane males. This conversation makes no sense to me at all." He turned to Cherry. "If you ever find out what Dr. Joe's idea is, let me know. I was just working up an interest in it."

"What's a séance?" Midge squeaked, and Mr. Ames bolted.

Séances—Dr. Joe's unrevealed plan—it was a crazy start to a crazy day.

First off, Cherry went downtown in search of Dr. Joe. Elderly, widowed Dr. Joseph Fortune held a unique place in Cherry's life. Neighbor, family doctor, friend, devoted researcher who often forgot meals, harrassed father of Midge, he had been "her" Dr. Joe, and her special concern, for many years. It was he who had opened for her the shining doors of humanitarian service through medicine. Ever since Cherry became a student nurse, in response to his inspiration, and in the gallant, hard-working years since, the elderly doctor and the young nurse had been doubly close.

Cherry found him at the new Hilton Clinic where, now that his days as an Army doctor were at an end, he was helping the sick both as physician and as medical researcher. He was, as usual, pottering around a wet, smelly laboratory table—a slight, appealing figure in a white lab coat, with that boyish shock of gray hair falling into one eye.

He looked up absently when a clinic attendant ushered Cherry in. "Just a minute, child, this slide is almost prepared—Ah! There." He delicately covered the little strip of glass, bearing a drop or two of fluid, with another glass slide, labeled it, and set it in the wooden rack. "A study in pneumonia germ," he explained, delight in his deep, slow voice. "A farm woman is ill with pneumonia. Well, well, my dear! Let's sit down and talk."

Cherry glanced at the two lab stools and the one chair, all piled high with scientific journals, half-smoked pipes, racks of test tubes. "I'll stand, thanks."

Dr. Joe looked around too. "Ah, yes. The desk isn't bad. I could push aside some of those papers. Or the radiator—that is unencumbered."

So they sat down together on the cold radiator.

"You always catch me at my same old tricks," Dr. Joe said. He shoved back the stubborn lock and smiled.

Cherry's dark eyes sparkled. "Midge reports you're up to a new trick—concerning me."

"Yes. I want you," said Dr. Joe, coming right to the point, "to have a try at private duty nursing."

STRANGE BEGINNING 9

"Nursing! Dr. Joe! Don't say nursing to me—I don't even want to think of it! And why private duty, of all things?"

"Because that farm woman I mentioned needs a nurse. She is at home, and we can't locate an R.N. to send out to her."

Cherry bent her curly head. The words of her nurse's pledge surged back: to serve wherever and whenever another human being needed her.

"Is it urgent?"

"Not terribly urgent. A rather light case, in fact. Her husband and her eight-year-old daughter are taking care of her. But the woman will recover more quickly and more thoroughly under a nurse's care."

"But, Dr. Joe, I don't know the first thing about private duty nursing!"

"There's nothing special to know, child. It's bedside nursing, the same as you've done in Spencer Hospital and in Army hospitals—only this time you nurse the patient in her own home."

"This comes with such a rush," Cherry gasped. "Of course, if you can't find another nurse—perhaps one who's done some private duty—"

Dr. Joe patted her reassuringly on the shoulder. "Don't worry about it, my dear. We'll try today to find another nurse. I think we'll find someone, all right."

"Aha!" said Cherry, sitting up very straight on the radiator. "First you offer me a case and then you say you'll get some other nurse! A fine thing! I mean it."

Dr. Joe chuckled. "But you don't know anything about private duty nursing, remember?"

"Then it may be high time I learned!"

"Well, think it over, Cherry. It's not urgent. I'm suggesting it mostly because I thought a taste of private duty, on a light case, might interest you."

Cherry rose, her cheeks flushed redder than ever. "You don't fool me with that casual tone, sir! Every time you make one mild, innocent little suggestion, I find myself in adventures up to my ears!"

Dr. Joe put his arm across her shoulders and walked her to the door. "As a matter of fact, I have a real adventure in mind for you."

"You have! I might have known! Oh, what is it?"

"I'd prefer not to tell you just yet. It might not materialize, and then you'd be disappointed."

"Stop tantalizing me—tell me even part of it!" Cherry begged.

"It's something big and interesting. Two or three or four private duty cases—short ones, here around Hilton—would be good preparation."

"Preparation for *what*? Oh, Dr. Joe—you meanie!"

Dr. Joe gently shoved her out into the hall. "Go away, monkey. I have to work. Good-bye." Laughing and shaking his gray head, Dr. Fortune shut the door on her.

STRANGE BEGINNING

Cherry opened the door a crack and hissed:

"You don't tempt me at all. I'm firmly determined to rest!"

And she marched out of the clinic, wishing she could believe that.

Certainly this warm June day invited relaxing. The whole town was in a summer mood. White shoes, straw hats, bright cotton dresses—baskets of nasturtium, fishing poles, sunburns, canvas tops of automobiles folded back—people lingering to chat in the sun and letting their business wait—children just freed from school for the summer, yelling in shrill voices—Cherry enjoyed Hilton in its easy summer mood. From these Middle West plains, stretching for flat, rich miles of farm land around Hilton, there rolled in the ripe fragrance of grain; the intense, hovering, inland heat of prairie; the hot, oily smell of gasoline—and Cherry breathed in the Illinois summer and loved it. She sauntered along, past the two- and three-story stores, past the ice-cream parlor where she sniffed fresh popcorn and crackerjack, poked her head into the ten-cent store on the chance that Midge might be in there grandly shopping.

Turning down quieter, leafy residential streets, Cherry's feet and not her volition brought her home. The last thing she remembered was a very sleepy lunch, then shooing a neighbor's kitten out of the hammock and tumbling into it herself.

The next thing Cherry knew, her mother was standing over her, hat and gloves on, murmuring:

"Poor baby, you're so tired out. I was going to ask you to come along to the séance—or at least come for the drive—but if you're too tired—"

Cherry announced that she was never too tired for nonsense, climbed into the back seat of Mrs. Pritchard's car, pondered where her early morning ambition had disappeared to, and promptly went to sleep again on Mrs. Ames's shoulder.

Her mother shook her gently, thirty miles later. They were pulling into Bluewater. This was a resort town, known for its restful lake and its music festivals. Plump Mrs. Pritchard, driving, and Mrs. McClay beside her welcomed Cherry back into their midst. Cherry apologized for having fallen asleep.

"Not sleep, dear. Call it a trance," her mother said smiling coyly. "Isn't that what we're going to see?"

"Heaven knows what claptrap we're going to see," Mrs. Pritchard joked back over her shoulder. "I expect to be swindled and enjoy it."

Mrs. McClay murmured that "there might be something in it," but the others laughed her down. In a mood of frank foolishness, the women parked before a shabby frame house and trooped in, like skylarking students. Cherry, bringing up the rear, felt herself the one staid and sensible member of their group.

STRANGE BEGINNING 13

She blinked on the darkened threshold. A stout, dignified woman of about forty came out of the shadows to meet them.

"I'm Mrs. Crawford," she said in a pleasant voice. She repeated their names: apparently they were expected. "Won't you come in and take seats, ladies? The room is closed off for quiet, but my landlady has electric fans going, so it should be cool. Yes, I'm in Bluewater for only a few weeks. Do come in."

Cherry stared at the woman. She had vaguely expected purple robes and turbans, but this fortuneteller was just an average-looking woman, with no hocus-pocus about her. She was quietly dressed, well-mannered, sympathetic—if anything, she was a shade too genteel. The only faintly gaudy thing about her was her fading, touched-up blonde hair. Even that, Cherry decided, was merely a pathetic effort to keep presentable.

"Please come in," she repeated. "The other ladies are waiting."

They groped their way into the darkened parlor. Cherry dimly saw three other women sitting around a bare table, in a circle of chairs. Mrs. Crawford seated Cherry next to an erect figure who, hat and all, in silhouette, bristled with efficiency. Then the fortuneteller closed the door, and they were in utter darkness.

The figure beside Cherry flashed a radium-dialed wrist watch. "We're seventeen minutes late in getting started. My word, that isn't practical!"

Cherry squelched a desire to inquire what a practical person thought she was doing at a ghost-raising party. But the woman added unexpectedly:

"Oh, well, maybe the spirits are still out to lunch."

Cherry giggled. Mrs. Crawford made a little disapproving sound. Cherry could feel the woman beside her holding back laughter.

But when Mrs. Crawford sat down at the table in creaking, ponderous stillness, they all quieted. The séance had started. Cherry knew that Mrs. Crawford had closed her eyes and was going into a trance, a sort of waking sleep in which she passively surrendered up her own will and identity to whatever might take possession of her. Ghosts?—not likely—or ideas floating up from the woman's subconscious. The trance was, Cherry knew, either a form of self-induced hypnosis or sheer fake.

They waited in solemn silence, Cherry dubious. The fortuneteller's breathing in the hot dark room grew louder, labored. They waited.

Mrs. Crawford rustled in her chair, and sighed heavily. "Eda—Eda—?" she gasped, in a high voice not at all like her own. "Wait—it's coming clearer—*Edith*."

Cherry heard her mother stir in her chair. The fortuneteller breathed noisily. The high, strained voice seemed torn out of her.

"Edith—Edith An— An— Yes, I'll speak for you, I'll speak!—Edith—*Anderly*!" Then, in her normal voice,

STRANGE BEGINNING

the medium said, "Is there anyone here named Edith Anderly?" The voice shifted back to the high, choked tones. "Charity Anderly—trying to get through—to—my daughter."

Mrs. Ames said in a subdued voice, "My name before my marriage was Edith Anderly. My mother's name was Charity."

Cherry's back tingled with gooseflesh, despite her disbelief. Her grandmother, Charity, had been dead for ten years.

From Mrs. Crawford came strained breathing. "Oh—oh—it's coming now—" The voice abruptly changed again, grew high and severe. "Edith. Edith. Don't sell your house. Don't do it. Stay where you are. Heed me. I can see more than you can."

A hush followed. Then the medium groaned and said exhaustedly, "She's gone." There was the tinkle of glass and ice as Mrs. Crawford apparently refreshed herself with a glass of water. In this interim, everyone relaxed a bit. Mrs. Pritchard whispered:

"Edith, I didn't know you were thinking of selling your home?"

"Yes, we were, vaguely," Mrs. Ames murmured back, to Cherry's surprise. Even Cherry had not known of it.

Mrs. Crawford asked, "Did you recognize your mother's voice, dear?"

"N-no. My mother's voice was pitched quite low."

"Oh? Well, of course, you see, the spirit voices are distorted in coming from the spirit world to this world, through the medium. Through me. I can only do my best, dear. Well, ladies! Shall we try again?"

The practical woman beside Cherry said solicitously, "If you feel rested enough to go into another trance?"

"You're always so considerate, Miss Owens. You're the most understanding of all my clients. Yes, I'm ready. Now let's all be quiet, while I concentrate."

Cherry slumped down in her chair, trying to decide what she thought of this shivery performance. Her common sense, her education, cried "Absurd!" Yet it was impressive and eerie, all the same.

Again the medium was still, then struggled to breathe, struggled to speak. Only broken syllables came. Cherry could see nothing, nothing, in this somber shadow. The tension mounted. The laboring woman in trance cried out sharply.

"Matthew! Matthew Austin— Yes —yes—" Then suddenly a deep voice, gruff as a man's, ripped out of her throat. "He's not here—no, no—But *she's* here! Dear, he's calling you! He wants to say—to tell—Matthew! He says—he never meant to—"

The woman beside Cherry screamed. A chair crashed to the floor. Running footsteps rang out, then the lights snapped on. The room was brightly visible in all its shabbiness. Miss Owens was standing near the door, her hand still trembling on the light switch. Cherry had her first look at her now: a badly scared woman, who

STRANGE BEGINNING 17

might have appeared pleasant and capable, even rather distinguished, at another moment. She held her other hand across her mouth, in a gesture of panic.

The expression on the other women's faces said plainly: "Silly woman—to take this seriously." Cherry summed up her reaction in one word: "Gullible." She felt rather sorry for the woman, too.

The medium was moaning, eyes half opening, startled out of her trance. Even to Cherry's trained, nurse's scrutiny, it was difficult to tell whether she was or was not faking that strange state. At any rate, she was nervous and shaken.

"How could you do such a thing?" she said indignantly to Miss Owens. "You of all people know how sensitive this work is—Dear, how could you play such havoc with my nerves?"

Miss Owens made apologies. Mrs. Crawford declared that after such a shock, she could not continue this afternoon. The other women paid her her fees, and left.

Out in the street and the sunshine, Cherry took a good, deep breath of fresh air. Nonsense or super-sense, she was relieved to escape from that dingy, stuffy place. Fortunetelling might be called entertainment, Cherry supposed, some people might take it seriously, and it was typical of an idle resort town like Bluewater. "But as for me, Bluewater can *keep* its vacationers and fortunetellers and music festivals!"

And so Cherry said later to Dr. Joe. He telephoned to invite her to a concert, that evening.

"What! Drive to Bluewater twice in the same day! Abandon our cool front porch? No, thank you, sir! Not even to hear the finest musician!" Cherry said heatedly into the telephone.

"Scott Owens *is* one of the finest musicians in this country," came back Dr. Joe's deep voice over the wire. "You don't want to miss him."

"Owens?" Cherry echoed. "I met a Miss Owens this afternoon. A nice-looking lady with—with an air. Lively. Reddish hair."

"Yes, the pianist's sister, Miss Kitty. His secretary and manager." Dr. Fortune explained that the celebrated pianist, a nervous man in precarious health, was resting for several weeks at Bluewater, under his sister's watchful eye. His recital tonight was unscheduled, a surprise performance to help raise benefit funds.

"And it's an event, Cherry, when Owens plays. People are coming down from Chicago on very short notice, for this recital. The big newspapers are flying their music critics down. Don't you want to come? I know him slightly and could introduce you."

"Dr. Joe, I'm sure it's worth while, because you aren't ordinarily so persistent. But please, please, let me off. I've had enough of Bluewater for one day!"

STRANGE BEGINNING

"Very well, child. But you might tune him in on your radio. Part of the program is being broadcast. I had planned—" Silence rang over the telephone wire.

"Planned what, Dr. Joe?"

"Nothing, nothing. Good night."

Cherry carelessly dismissed the whole matter.

An hour later she turned on the radio. Leaving her parents reading in the blue-and-mahogany living room, with the doors open to the summer night, she sauntered out to the porch. The porch, with its flowering clematis and honeysuckle vines, was like an island of fragrance in the evening world of shadows. Cherry curled up in the swing.

For a few moments she half listened to radio voices, blurred announcements, enjoying her seclusion. Then a torrent of ravishing music burst on the night air. Cherry lay transfixed, listening, overwhelmed. Never had she heard such gorgeousness—such full-throated violins and cellos, such deep and insistent horns, such rich weavings of melody, or—singing pure and alone above all the rest—such crystalline waterfall notes of piano. Cascades of music swelled and dreamed and soared around her.

Cherry listened, bewitched and transported, and completely forgot such mundane things as nursing.

CHAPTER II

R.F.D.

THE PHONE RANG EARLY IN THE MORNING. IT WAS DR. JOE.

"Cherry, you *have* to take that farm case. The patient is worse. We can't locate a registered nurse to send out there. Get packed. I'll be over in ten minutes to explain."

Cherry's black curls were still tousled, her face still flushed from sleep. She hopped into a cold shower to wake up, and dressed at top speed, thinking furiously. She knew nothing about private duty nursing! But she was a nurse—a sick woman needed her—and nursing was nursing, whether Cherry did it in a hospital or made a specialty of it in someone's home. As she scampered about her room, getting out a small suitcase and thermometers and a white uniform, she felt real excitement. This would be the first time she nursed on her own, without ranks of doctors and nursing supervisors and superintendents to guide her! The whole responsibility for a woman's life and health fell on her alone. Cherry vowed that, even though no one but the single doctor on the case would drop by occasionally to check up on her work, *her* private duty nursing, in some obscure bedroom, would be every bit as good as in the finest hospital.

What equipment to take along, to care for her patient? Cherry hurriedly dug in her closet through professional magazines and leaflets from the American Nurses' Association of which she was a member. Here! Here was just the information she needed! Blessings on the ANA for coming to her rescue.

"PRIVATE DUTY NURSES PLEASE NOTE—

Instruments	Watch with second hand
Probe	Glass hypodermic syringe
Tissue forceps	Large needles
Grooved director	Small needles
Scissors	Thermometers
Hemostat	Uniform
Flashlight	Patient's record blanks"

Yes, Cherry believed she had all these items but she would have to locate them. In the future, she would keep her kit already packed for instant readiness! She slammed drawers open and shut. The doorbell rang downstairs. Dr. Joe already! Her mother was calling:

"For goodness' sake, what's happening here?"

Cherry raced out to the staircase and called down, "Mother, you just aren't used to having a nurse in the household! I'm going out on a case!"

Dr. Joe, coming in, smiled. "Never a dull moment in a medical household, Mrs. Ames. May I go upstairs? While Cherry packs, I can talk to her about the case. It will save us precious time."

The unceremonious doctor climbed up to Cherry's topsy-turvy room. Mrs. Ames brought a pot of coffee. Cherry flew about getting her bag packed, but listened carefully to Dr. Fortune.

The patient was Mrs. Jessie Tucker, young wife of a farmer, and mother of several small children. She worked hard on the farm, had grown overtired, caught cold and neglected it. Result: pneumonia, even in the summertime. For a week, Mrs. Tucker had been in Hilton Hospital, attended by a private duty nurse. Dr. Joe paused to explain that most private nurses "specialed" individual cases in hospitals; only about ten per cent of them were called to nurse in patients' homes. In the hospital, Mrs. Tucker had passed the crisis of her illness and improved enough to be sent home.

"They couldn't afford the heavy expenses of hospital and private nurse," Dr. Joe said. "We tried to get her home quickly for that reason. Also, she was worrying herself literally sick about those neglected children at home."

"Then they can't afford *me* either?"

"Not very well, Cherry. But they can't afford *not* to have a nurse. Mrs. Tucker's husband and neighbors have done their best in nursing her but she has had a relapse. There has to be a real nurse in charge."

Cherry made a mental note to charge the Tuckers as little as possible for her services. Her sympathies for this young farm family were already aroused—and a houseful of youngsters should be fun!

"I'm glad you're the doctor on the case, Dr. Joe."

"But I'm not. I was merely one of the consulting doctors at the hospital. Dr. Birdwell is the one. He's a real, old-fashioned, country doctor. Don't underestimate him—"

Jogging out to Dr. Birdwell's in the country, in an interurban streetcar, Cherry thought over all that Dr. Joe had said. She tried, too, to get straight in her mind exactly what her nursing responsibility would encompass. To carry out Dr. Birdwell's orders—medication, treatment, diet. To watch her patient constantly and recognize any SOS change in her condition. To keep the sufferer as comfortable and cheerful as possible. "And probably," Cherry thought, "to soothe and encourage the whole Tucker brood!"

"Lawrenceville!" the conductor sang out.

Cherry straightened her neat plaid cotton dress, clapped her big straw hat on the back of her head, and kit in hand, alighted. Lawrenceville consisted of a filling station, a grocery, and two chickens in the road.

No Dr. Birdwell, no Mr. Tucker, was on hand to meet the nurse who had come to save them all. Not even the sauntering chickens were impressed.

Cherry gulped. A promising start to her new career! She went into the weather-beaten grocery. Three old men stared at her. Also present was a small dirty boy with a goat.

"I'm the nurse for Mrs. Tucker," Cherry said. "Could you tell me, please, how to get to Dr. Birdwell's, and then to the Tucker farm?"

Silence. What they lacked in eloquence, Cherry thought, they certainly made up in suspicion. "Nurse" to them clearly meant something fancy and totally unnecessary.

Cherry tried again. "Which way to Dr. Birdwell's?"

The small boy fidgeted. Then he bent down and twisted the goat's tail. The goat protested. There was silence again, as the local deadpans stood like carved figures.

"See here," Cherry demanded angrily, "there's a sick woman to take care of! Are you going to direct me or not?"

"Two mile due north," grudged the smallest of the old men, and limped off.

"Can I hire someone to drive me there?"

Several pairs of hostile eyes consulted one another. No one looked at Cherry. Finally a hatchet-faced man spoke to the ceiling.

"Five dollars. Pay in advance."

Cherry walked. She arrived hot, dusty, and exasperated. But Dr. Birdwell's house, perched in the middle of nowhere, cheered her up. Outside, it was rambling, shabby, and covered with flowering vines. Inside, the rooms were cool and primly old-fashioned. The doctor's elderly wife gave her a glass of ice-cold buttermilk, to cool off with, and said:

"The doctor'll be to home right soon. You jest set."

So Cherry "jest set," and chuckled at the foolish cuckoo bobbing out of the clock, and puzzled over backwoods ways. If people here did not welcome a nurse, preferring neighbors' care and home remedies and even old superstitions to up-to-date medical techniques, what a job this country doctor must have on his hands!

He came bustling in, a rosy old man, a bit tired but in high good humor. His bushy white hair, his gold-rimmed spectacles, his worn black kit, were exactly what Cherry had expected. But she had not foreseen the shrewdness in his eyes.

"Yes, Miss Cherry, folks around here, some of 'em, distrust newfangled ideas. Not all the folks, only the older ones. You and I, we have a job to do, to educate 'em." Cherry smiled at him for that "you and I," for generously including her with himself, a doctor and a wise, experienced old man.

The country doctor smiled back and said, "Matter of fact, a peart young 'un like you, just fresh out of Army

Nurse Corps and used to all the newest, smart-alecky ways—I'll bet you're going to turn up your nose at some of the old fogy ways I do things." He sighed a little and polished his spectacles. "I try to study and keep up with all the new discoveries. But with this whole stretch of countryside to keep healthy, I'll tell you, it keeps me hoppin'. These folks can't pay me much, so I can't afford to buy all the grandest new equipment, neither. I do the best I humanly can, that's all. That's the most a man can do."

Cherry said softly, "I guess human understanding is at least as important as a shiny new stethoscope."

Dr. Birdwell laughed heartily. "Sis, you and me're going to get along fine! I can see that!"

He instructed her about the pneumonia case she was to handle. Jessie Tucker must be given sulfa every four hours around the clock, exactly on the hour. She needed a light, nourishing diet, but not a special diet, particularly—"anything that appeals to her, exceptin' eggs and greasy things. Coax her to eat, Sis." Cherry was to keep the patient warm, using a hot-water bottle on the patient's stomach, center of the circulatory system. "Don't know as the Tuckers own a hot-water bottle. You'll have to find substitutes as you go along. Say, you know," he chuckled, "a cat is warm and soft, sittin' on you and snoozin'. But the durn cat won't always stay put!" If the sulfa gave Jessie Tucker headaches, Dr. Birdwell ordered an ice pack or cold compresses on her forehead. Cherry was especially to watch the patient's temperature, and if it soared, to notify the physician at once. "And if anything goes wrong, holler for me and nurse like a house afire!"

And with these highly informal and colorful instructions, Cherry set off in Dr. Birdwell's rickety car for the Tucker farm.

Cherry asked the doctor to make one strategic stop on the way, for ice cream.

Out of growing fields rose a white frame house, shaded by oak trees. A little farther off, by a red barn, four children played. As Dr. Birdwell's auto chugged up, they came running, followed by an ancient dog, a tomcat, a pig which apparently had been let out of its pen, and a tame hen. One toddler was so small its legs could barely keep pace with the hen.

"Hello, kids!" the white-haired doctor called. "This is Miss Cherry, come to help your ma get well."

Cherry grinned at the assorted children. They gazed back at her solemnly, as Dr. Birdwell named them. First came Ruth, a girl of about eight, with pigtails and a responsible scowl. Ruth was mothering the brood. Then came Sam, six, and Susie, five, a pair of devils covered with dust and bliss, busy blowing saliva bubbles. The staggering one-and-a-half-year-old, nondescript in rompers, turned out to be a boy, nicknamed Sparky. The new baby, Marietta, three months, of whom Sparky was frankly jealous, was in the care of a kindly neighbor, away from the infectious pneumonia. All the children, with their mother ill, were in various states of disrepair.

"Hi," said Cherry, speculating how best to win over this suspicious little crowd. She foresaw that half of her nursing job here might be scrubbing, feeding, and keeping these children from falling out of trees, setting the house afire, or running off with the team of horses. Her plan to wear starchy white from head to toe faded with one glance at Sam climbing astride the pig.

"Hi," said Cherry again, and gulped.

There was a long, hostile pause. There were glares from four round pairs of eyes.

"Hi," Ruth grudged finally. She pointed to the tomcat. "That's Mary Alice. The dog is Bobo. He lost part of his tail. The hen is Mrs. Jones. The pig is just pig."

"They're awfully nice pets," Cherry replied. Silence closed down again like measles. Cherry looked around for Dr. Birdwell to come to her rescue. His coattails were just flapping into the house.

"How's your mother today?"

"She's sick." Followed by echoes . . . "Sick, didn't you know that?" "You don't know nuthin'."

"I'm going to help her get well, real soon."

"Huh." Echoed by Sam's and Susie's smaller grunts.

"Ahhh—Mary Alice is a pretty cat."

More silence. Cherry went to Dr. Birdwell's car and produced a large cardboard container.

"Who wants ice cream?"

Whoops of joy greeted this. The children scrambled around Cherry, beaming at her. The new nurse via large scoops of ice cream won a diplomatic victory.

Cherry hurried after Dr. Birdwell into the house. Every room looked, in his phrase, "like a cyclone struck it." The only room free of joyous disorder was the darkened quiet bedroom, upstairs, where Jessie Tucker lay.

She was still young, round-faced, with brown hair streaming over her shoulders and the counterpane. She would have been pretty except for her fretful expression. When Dr. Birdwell led Cherry to her bedside, she turned her head away.

"I don't want any strange woman around here, runnin' my house and my childern. I don't want any outsiders buttin' in on this family."

"Now, Jess," the old doctor clucked.

Cherry felt a sting of hurt, then resentment. But quickly she put the brake on her emotions, set her mind going instead. Any intelligent nurse, she knew, made allowance for a patient's becoming irritable or fearful or impatient. Why, those reactions were as much a symptom of illness as this woman's paleness or the limp, exhausted way she lay propped on the pillows. Jessie Tucker might be an entirely different person when she was well and herself. So Cherry was undismayed, and said:

"I'm here to nurse you, my dear. If you *want* me to keep an eye on your youngsters, then tell me what to do—and I'll carry out your orders exactly."

The patient studied Cherry with feverish eyes. "Don't let Sam play with the Norton boy. He's a bad one. Keep Sam home."

"All right, I will."

"I've been lyin' here in bed worryin' about Sam."

Dr. Birdwell said, "Worry'll keep you from getting well, Jess. Stop worrying and let your nurse take charge."

Mrs. Tucker looked somewhat mollified but still uneasy. Dr. Birdwell gave Cherry a few minor instructions, jollied the sick woman, and departed.

Now Cherry tied on an apron, washed her hands in a china basin, and turned to her patient. Four small curious faces watched from the doorway. Cherry gently sent them outdoors. She opened her kit and looked around the room for articles she would need.

"What're you going to do to me?" Jessie Tucker demanded. "No, you don't!"

"I have to take your pulse, temperature, and respiration—breathing rate. Then I'll give you a nice bed bath and remake your bed. You'll feel fresh, then, for lunch and your afternoon rest."

"My bed's all right. Don't want any lunch. Oh, leave me alone!"

The new nurse found herself in the embarrassing position of being unable to get near her patient. Too, the four inquisitive faces had popped right back in the doorway, like four jacks-in-the-box. Six-year-old Sam danced into the bedroom, tugging his own hair, and sang:

"Hay foot! Straw foot! Belly full of beans!"

Ruth grabbed him. He pulled her pigtails. They tussled. Susie piped, "More ice cream! More!" Mrs. Tucker paled and trembled.

"Out with you!" Cherry said, and stampeded the small gang out of the sickroom and down the stairs. She would have shut the door but knew instinctively that the children's mother wanted that door left open. She approached her patient with a thermometer and firmness.

"I'm not used to bein' fussed over," Mrs. Tucker started. But while her mouth was open, Cherry popped the thermometer in. Simultaneously she took the sick woman's wrist, counted pulse, then counted breathing. Hastily scribbling out a chart, Cherry recorded the too-high T.P.R. "Now for the bed bath," she bluffed, as if that were a settled matter, and looked around for a fresh pitcher of water or a sink. This farmhouse had no such conveniences.

There were, however, Ruth, Sam, and Susie, back in the doorway. Sparky and the hen peeked in between their knees. Cherry experienced exasperation, amusement, impending catastrophe and, suddenly, inspiration.

"Come out in the hall with me," she whispered. "For a conference."

Wide-eyed, the children gathered around her.

"Do you want your mama to get well?" Their anxious nods were pitiful. "Will you be my helpers?" Eager nods. "Sam, I appoint you Officer of the Home Guard. You stand guard around the house, understand?" The little fellow nodded importantly. "Susie, I appoint you special helper in charge of—um—the mail." Susie did not look overjoyed, so Cherry added, "And I appoint you to tell Sparky a story at the same time—if you can manage two jobs." Susie stood up straighter. Sparky merely patted the chicken, his friend. "Ruth, I appoint you my personal assistant. Please bring me a kettle of warm water and some towels."

The children scurried off. At last Cherry's work was under way.

The bed bath went off smoothly, and the patient seemed refreshed and relaxed afterwards. Cherry gave her sulfa, at the exact minute. A neighbor brought over hot food. Cherry delegated Ruth to serve it to the children. She herself rummaged in the kitchen, prepared a light, appetizing tray for the invalid, and coaxed her to eat. Then she made Mrs. Tucker comfortable for a nap, and went downstairs feeling she had earned a bite of lunch herself.

Mr. Tucker had come in from the fields, to meet the new nurse. John Tucker was a big, sunburned, raw-boned man in blue jeans, hearty and friendly. He pumped Cherry's hand.

"Sure is a relief to have you here, miss," he boomed. "Well, you just take over and I'll see you at suppertime."

Cherry blinked. A great help *he* was going to be! Man-fashion, he had little idea of all the chores involved in managing house, children, an invalid. "Just take over—!" Cherry shook her black curls and suddenly burst out laughing. Private duty nursing apparently meant—here at least—playing foster mother, housekeeper, cook—and nursing when and if there was any time left over.

Cherry did not bat an eyelash. She pitched in, and without feeling any loss of professional dignity, either. If Florence Nightingale at Scutari did not hesitate to act as messenger, housecleaner, nurse, treasurer, and insect exterminator, then Cherry Ames need not feel any false pride either!

Absolutely first came care of the patient. The children's mother submitted grumblingly to more sulfa, and to a hot mustard plaster treatment, but she did submit. Cherry observed her condition closely that afternoon and charted it. She found it difficult, in this house without running water or electrical appliances and with steep stairs, to keep fresh water in the bedside pitcher—to sterilize glasses and rubber gloves after using them—to bring up orange juice at four o'clock and a supper tray at six. Eight-year-old Ruth thought of a good plan. She and Cherry rigged up a basket, tied it to a stout cord from the upper railing of the stairway, and used it as a freight elevator, with Ruth on call downstairs. It was crude but it saved Cherry many steps.

All afternoon and evening, Cherry labored to systematize her work, and failed. But she learned a valuable lesson: a private duty nurse, coming into a household already confused by illness, needs a day or two to adjust herself to a new patient and the ways of a new house-hold. "Tomorrow," Cherry promised herself, "I'll sit down quietly and plan out various routine duties I have to do during the day, and schedule them. I've done my gosh darnedest for the first day!"

She yawned and suddenly realized—now that the whole family had gone to bed—that she herself had no designated place to sleep. Oh, my! Put a cot in Mrs. Tucker's room? Roost on the couch downstairs? No, no. Uncomfortable and no privacy. Well, *where*? Cherry's heart sank. Had no one remembered to make provision for the nurse?

Ruth had. The eight-year-old, in a long white nightgown, beckoned Cherry out of the sickroom.

"I fixed up the spare chamber for you," she whispered. "I aired the room and dusted and made the bed— all by myself!"

"Ruthie, you are a friend in need."

"I'm your personal assistant, aren't I?"

Sulfa to give Mrs. Tucker at midnight, at four A.M., again at eight next morning—up and down all night—Cherry decided to dress more warmly than if she were going to bed to stay there. Yet in order to feel rested in the morning, she must get this plaid cotton dress and these shoes off. In the spare bedroom, she took a quick sponge bath, donned fresh underthings, fresh stockings, and her robe. She put her slippers near by and handy. Now she lay down with the door open, the alarm clock set for midnight and the first night dose, and one ear alert. In the morning she would try to squeeze in another sponge bath, and would change her clothes again. It was a broken-up night. Yet Cherry managed to sleep, and awakened refreshed.

The next day went serenely, and so did the days that followed. Cherry rarely saw Mr. Tucker, who worked a long day at his tractor and plow. She kept a watchful eye on the children when she could, but the helpful neighbors fed them and Ruth supervised them. So Cherry spent the bulk of her time in the sickroom, after all. Jessie Tucker's improvement was gratifying. Cherry tactfully wore away the young woman's objections, and helped her via medicine, treatments, good food, gentle care, and her own personal encouragement. Her fever died away to a normal temperature, her lung congestion was clearing up rapidly. Dr. Birdwell came in once each day, for half an hour, and seemed well satisfied with the results of Cherry's nursing.

The days slid by, melting into one another, calm, efficient, under control. The baby, Marietta, was sent home, adding heavily to Cherry's chores. But Cherry still shivered when she recalled the bedlam she had had to conquer on her arrival. The actual nursing was the least of a private nurse's problems! Cherry felt some pride in the way she had evolved order from chaos. She had achieved it apparently without being a martinet, for the whole Tucker family liked her and Sparky called her "Harry dear."

"I want to see my mama!" Susie proclaimed, with Sam roaring and Sparky lisping the same demand.

Cherry knew that their mother wanted to see them, too, and that it would speed her recovery. So she announced visiting hours (for small fry only), and to enforce them she handed out tickets. The price of admission was good behavior. Sam wriggled in twice on one ticket, but otherwise the system worked perfectly. True, Jessie Tucker was worn out after listening to assorted gabblings about mud pies, the pig, Marietta's faults (this from Susie), and dozens of questions. But Cherry counted her fatigue as good, healthy preparation for a nap. She did not permit the children to stay long enough really to exhaust the convalescing patient.

One of Cherry's daily jobs was bathing three-months-old Marietta, on the kitchen table. She was an amiable baby, and this would have been no trouble, except that the whole troupe of youngsters wanted to "help." Cherry was uncertain whether she could handle four rough-and-tumble children, hold on to a soapy, slippery baby, and have everybody emerge in one piece. But, loving children, she was willing to try.

"Sam!"

"Yes'm?" The Home Guard Officer came to attention.

"You may fetch water for the baby's bath. You and Ruth will heat it to lukewarm. Susie! I'm going to trust you to bring the baby's clean clothes and arrange them in exactly the right order."

Three of them scampered off. Sparky stood unsteadily in baggy rompers, not understanding anything except that, forlornly, he was left out.

"Sparky, you talk nicely to the baby and help rub its back."

"Yesh, Harry dear."

Filling the tub from the water kettle was so popular that each child had to have a turn. Then each one had his own special part of the program, which he took pride in carrying out well. Susie was soap and washcloth bearer, and she did *not* drip. Sam was towel and talcum bearer. Ruth held the baby in sitting position in the tub, and helped dress her. Sparky was trusted to examine and "test" each article in the baby's basket, putting each back in its place. When the ceremony was all over, there were happy, satisfied remarks of, "We was a real help." "Yes, and just think! We get to do it all over again tomorrow!" "Gee whiz, a whole day to wait."

By the end of the week, Mrs. Tucker was sitting up in bed and asking for something to do. Cherry used ingenuity to break the monotony of convalescence. She brought crocheting, magazines, permitted neighbors to pay short calls. She herself talked to the family's mother about hygiene and preventive health measures. For any nurse is a health missionary. Cherry also showed Ruth and, when she could catch him, Mr. Tucker, how to feed their patient, take temperature, lift her from bed to rocking chair, against the time the nurse left.

Cherry had made everything ready for the doctor's daily visit—the patient comfortable and tidy after morning care, the room dusted and straightened, the chart of the patient's reactions up to the minute, thermometer and fresh towels at hand. She stood up when Dr. Birdwell entered, as a mark of nurse's professional respect for a doctor—the same medical etiquette she would have observed in a hospital.

"Good morning, good morning!" the country doctor sang out. He looked like Santa Claus in a black suit. He briefly examined the patient and said, "Jessie, you're getting well so fast, you won't let me make any money on you."

Jessie Tucker smiled, and looked toward Cherry. "My nurse has been mighty good to me. To my childern too. I'm thankful to her."

"You don't think any more that you need a private nurse 'about as much as you need a third leg'?" Dr. Birdwell teased. "Well, I'm thankful to Miss Cherry myself. Not often I get a nurse to help me—many's the time I make a poultice or change a dressing myself. Jess, I couldn't 've saved you just with pills and visits. I'll tell you now that it's all over, you might've gone out of here in a long box, feet first, if it hadn't been for this nurse."

Cherry's cheeks turned very pink indeed at his praise. Hayseed, old fogy methods, or no, Cherry esteemed this wise and kindly old doctor. She also felt embarrassed enough to sink through the floor, right onto the table where they scrubbed Marietta.

"Rise and shine, Jess! Rise and shine!" said Dr. Birdwell. "And you, young lady, you can pack your duds any day now and get along home."

Cherry felt genuinely sorry to be leaving them. In the week since that awful day she arrived, Cherry had grown into the Tucker clan and farm. John Tucker wrung her hand until it hurt and thanked her "for a bang-up job." Jessie Tucker admitted she was sorry "for bein' a mite cranky that first day—and you drive out for Sunday supper, hear?" The children all but went into mourning. For Cherry had understood they were not actually demons, could do valiant deeds like washing a baby, and were hollow to the toes.

One last, small problem was left. What was Cherry to charge the Tuckers for her services? She had not the heart to ask regular fees, for the crops which helped feed a nation barely kept these sprouting, button-bursting children in hand-me-downs and corn bread.

"I'll tell you what," she said finally to Mrs. Tucker. Her bag was packed and Susie was hanging on to her skirt. "I'd like to take some of the farm back to town with me. Pay me in produce."

So John Tucker and the children loaded her down with jellies and jams, two hens and a bag of feed, and a bushel of cherries for pies. Dr. Birdwell squeezed all of this, and Cherry, and his plump self, into his ramshackle auto.

The whole Tucker family waved. Sam stood on his head. With a grand sputter, the auto jerked forward and Cherry was off.

CHAPTER III

Do, Re, Mi and Company

"WELL, DR. JOE? WELL? DID THE TUCKERS TEACH ME enough or do I—and some patient—have to suffer some more?"

They were in Dr. Joe's laboratory at the clinic. It was a hot morning, with the atmosphere ready to burst. Cherry felt about to burst, herself—with curiosity and restlessness.

"Suffer to what purpose?" Dr. Joe inquired mildly, looking over his mail.

"You said I have to acquire experience—preparation—great wisdom and so on—before you pronounce me ready for that mysterious future!"

Dr. Joe peered at her over his reading glasses. "You'd see a mystery in anything, monkey. There's nothing mysterious about the plan I have in mind for you."

"Then *what is it*? Please!"

But Dr. Joe would not tell her, not yet. Cherry went home and worked on something new, cross but determined.

Since she was, really, in business for herself now, she had better behave like a business woman. Sitting cross-legged on her couch-bed in her red-and-white room, surrounded by a sea of papers, Cherry played business woman. She importantly printed CHERRY AMES, R.N., in her record book. The book looked impressively professional.

Then Cherry pondered what information her record book should include. After consulting the American Nurses' Association leaflets, and learning in ten minutes what experienced private duty nurses had sifted out after being battered by many cases, Cherry lettered in these items:

DATE OF RECEIVING CALL AND DATE LEFT CASE: *June 5–12*
DIAGNOSIS: *Pneumonia*
LOCATION OF CASE: *Patient's home, outside Hilton*
PATIENT'S NAME: *Mrs. Jessie Tucker*
DOCTOR'S NAME: *Dr. Birdwell*
SOURCE OF CALL:

Here Cherry paused. The leaflet read "called by registry, doctor, et cetera." Well, she had not been engaged for this case through a registry nor through et cetera. She scribbled in. "Through Dr. Fortune," and came to a decision. She had better get her name in at a nurses' registry, if she wanted more calls—pending Dr. Joe's "mysterious future" for her! She would have to ask Dr. Joe how a registry worked.

FEE EARNED: Cherry paused again. Heavens, she was budgeting not only her earnings but (when she came to think of it) her living expenses, savings, vacations—her whole life! Cocking her curly head, she said to the record book:

"You haven't any love interest—you're not even a glamorous memory book—but you certainly are exciting in your way! And you certainly are going to come in handy!"

Cherry's imagination immediately darted from the prosaic business uses of her record book to more dramatic ways it might figure: as evidence in a trail over a mysterious death, its causes disputed—as a clue in tracking down a poisoning— She caught herself and laughed, and went on to setting up such businesslike papers as statements (or bills, to be presented to her patients), receipts, and a small file for keeping track of her total earnings. Cherry fairly bristled with efficiency and importance during these operations.

Finally Dr. Joe telephoned. "Cherry, it's all arranged."

"*What's* all arranged?"

"You're going with Scott Owens."

"Scott O— Just like that, Dr. Joe?"

"Yes, just like that, my dear. Can you come over here?"

44   CHERRY AMES, PRIVATE DUTY NURSE

Now Cherry found out what her new adventure was to be and why Dr. Fortune had pressed her to go to that unscheduled recital. That evening he had made an engagement, far in advance, for Nurse Ames to take Scott Owens's case. Delays, last-minute changes in the musician's plans, had kept Dr. Joe from telling Cherry about it until he was sure. Now Scott Owens wanted her, tomorrow. Not in Bluewater but in Owens's big midwest city.

The pianist was not sick-abed but he often did have heart attacks and fall ill. His chronic heart condition required more watchful and expert care than Miss Kitty, his sister, could give him. Cherry would act as nurse companion to the pianist and his sister, watching Scott Owens for symptoms of acute attack, giving medication, trying to keep her patient physically quiet and emotionally undisturbed. Also, the Owenses traveled a great deal on concert tours, and Cherry would go along.

"It isn't the soft job it sounds," Dr. Joe said, "for Owens is an artist and a highly nervous, active person. You will be called upon to use all your tact."

Next morning, Cherry raced around her room packing her medical instruments in their kit. Another suitcase stood open for her clothes. Her mother checked over Cherry's wardrobe, pressing, tightening a loose button, rejecting a faded blouse. Midge was downtown having all Cherry's shoes shined and reheeled. Her father was getting her railroad ticket. Cherry had two last-minute chores which no one else could do for her. One was to get herself immaculately bathed, shampooed, groomed, and dressed with a little style. The other was to register at the central nurses' directory. Dr. Joe had said the Owens case might not last. If Cherry wanted more calls for private duty work, she had better register.

Cherry hastened downtown in the blistering heat. The nurses' registry was a businesslike office with a huge switchboard. Doctors telephoned here to engage private duty nurses, taking whichever nurse was next on the registry's waiting list. Or a doctor or a patient could ask the registry to send his own favorite nurse. Cherry paid a fee, reported herself ready for duty after the Owens case, agreed to obey the directory's rules, and to answer willingly and promptly any calls they telephoned to her. She had the privilege of registering for or against any certain class of cases—maternity or pneumonia or long heart cases—but decided not to specialize. The middle-aged nurse who ran the registry told her, "You'll have dry spells of telephone watching. But don't let a dull season throw you into a panic. Five days of work this month—twenty days next month—it evens up in the end."

At home her mother had completed the packing for her. Mr. Ames and Midge returned for a hasty farewell lunch. But since Cherry would be near Hilton, no elaborate good-byes were said. Besides, her thoughts strained forward to the colorful people, the unknown house, which would fill her life.

It was a tall narrow city house, of stone, on a bustling city street. Cherry stood before it, a few hours later, in the hot afternoon, and wondered what lay behind the tall curtained windows on each of its four floors. From somewhere on an upper floor came the sound of a piano, fitful, stopping, starting again.

Cherry stood listening. An organ grinder with a monkey came around the corner, mopping his brow. He set down his hand organ before the Owens house and started to grind. An off-key, squeaky version of *I Love You* shrilled out.

The piano stopped. A window flew up. A man's agitated face peered out.

"Go away! Please go away! How often must I tell you that noise drives me mad?"

The organ grinder grinned blandly, looked up. Cherry looked up too. The clamorous hand organ ground on. The man at the window was replaced by the reddish haired woman Cherry had seen at the séance. She called down calmly:

"If I give you a dollar will you go away?"

"Two dollars."

"For two dollars you stay away."

"A' right." The music stopped. The organ grinder winked at Cherry. "Poor fella. He don't like music."

Miss Owens came running down the narrow house steps. For a tall and buxom middle-aged woman, she

DO, RE, MI AND COMPANY 47

was surprisingly light and quick. She seemed as calm as the man had been disturbed, and disposed of the organ grinder with firmness.

"He'll be back next week," she said to Cherry with a laugh. "Oh, hello!" she exclaimed, suddenly aware of Cherry's presence. "Aren't you our nurse? A fine way to receive you, Miss Cherry Ames—on the street. And we've been looking forward so eagerly to your arrival!" All the while she was talking, she was intently studying Cherry's face. "I just know I've met you before," she rattled on. "Now, let me see. Where could it have been?"

Cherry started to recall to her the séance at Bluewater, when the realization of where they had met suddenly dawned on the woman. Cherry was startled by the look of agitation that swept over her face.

"Oh, dear!" she exclaimed. "Now I know. It was at Mrs. Crawford's séance—that horrible day when Uncle Matthew—" she shuddered. "But never mind that now," she shrugged off the feeling of horror abruptly.

Linking her arm through Cherry's, she picked up one of Cherry's bags, and cordially shoved her into the house. She talked the whole time, about the séance, the heat, her brother, Cherry's fabulous red cheeks. Cherry grinned and liked Miss Kitty Owens.

They entered a long, high-ceilinged living room, dominated by a concert grand piano. In the wide archway leading to a similar room beyond, stood another grand piano which backed up to the first.

"For two-piano scores," Miss Kitty said. "Is it awfully warm in here? I've kept the house darkened all day. Do sit down and I'll have Jen bring us iced tea or something. Oh, Jen! Jen! There, Scott's playing again—he has a practice room upstairs, I was afraid the organ grinder had stopped him. Sit down on the couch, there aren't any chairs, just couches."

Cherry groped through the half light to the nearest big divan, littered with pillows of all colors. She sat down, settling herself against the pillows. They felt much too warm and solid, then suddenly they snapped at her. They were three dirty-white poodles.

"That's Do, Re, Mi," said Miss Kitty. "Everybody sits down on them sooner or later. Ignore them."

Cherry patted the three indignant poodles. They glared at her. Suddenly she felt someone watching her and whirled around to face a pair of deep, brooding eyes. She blinked in the shadows and refocused. The eyes seemed to stare at her from the white marble mantel, from between marble busts of Beethoven and Mozart.

"That's Octave the cat," said Miss Owens. "Can't very well call him Kitty, ha, ha! A yellow Persian. Don't ignore *him,* you'll hurt his catly pride. Ah, Jen. That looks refreshing."

A motherly gray-haired woman had come up from the basement kitchen with a tray of iced drinks. She nodded at Cherry as Miss Owens introduced them, and said candidly:

"I hope you like music and don't mind musicians. Otherwise you'll never survive here. But once you get used to it, it's not bad."

"Go 'long with you, Jen," Miss Kitty said affectionately.

"Miss Kitty and I have managed to preserve our sanity," the woman said to Cherry. "I can't say as much for my husband. Do you know what Lucien has been doing all afternoon?"

"Seeing to that repair on the car?" Miss Owens asked hopefully.

"Over in the park practicing on the flute. He must think he's Pan. At his age! That's your brother's doing. Mr. Scott told him a flute had best be played in the open air." She picked up the tray and smiled dryly at Cherry. "Good luck, young lady."

Miss Kitty chuckled as Jen left. Cherry was still recovering from her amusement when her employer plunged into a discussion of practical details. Cherry would have a room on the third floor, the guest floor. In fact, Cherry was welcome to the whole third floor just now, if she could think of anything to do with it. The ample basement housed Jen and Lucien; here were the living rooms on the street floor. Miss Kitty's bedroom, her office, and Mr. Scott's bedroom, were on the second floor. The third was Cherry's. On the fourth floor, the pianist had his practice room and a study. Cherry was curious to see those. In back of the house, Miss Kitty showed her from the big rear windows, was a small, city back yard, carpeted with green grass, ornamented with one showering mulberry tree.

And throughout all this conversation ran like water the limpid, precise percussion of the piano upstairs. It punctuated everything, their talk, their mood, their breathing, even the walls seemed faintly to ring with music. Echoes went singing on after the music itself had ceased.

A thin, almost gaunt man walked into the living room. He had one of the kindest, gentlest faces Cherry had ever seen.

"Oh, Scott!" his sister said. "I wanted you to welcome Miss Cherry, but I hated to interrupt your work."

"How do you do, Miss Cherry," he said and she looked up into bottomless eyes. His voice, like his slow walk, his uncompleted gestures, was weak. "There's a frail person," Cherry thought. "And a sweet one," as his smile glowed from deep in his eyes and slowly lighted up his face. He sat down abstractedly, apologized because his trousers and jacket did not match, hoped Cherry would be happy here, and went off into a sort of waking dream. A second later he said shyly:

"May I ask you something?"

"Of course, anything, Mr. Owens." She expected a question about his health or her nursing.

"Mr. Scott," he corrected. "Do you play? You had a few lessons when you were a child? Very well, then, let's hear you."

DO, RE, MI AND COMPANY   51

Cherry opened her mouth to protest. Play before a concert artist! She had never played really well—had not practiced for years—But Miss Kitty was making faces at her, and her patient was waiting. Cherry went to the nearest piano.

"You'll be sorry," she muttered before she could stop the words. They both laughed.

She played, as best her fingers could remember it, a simple Chopin waltz.

"That's awful," said Scott Owens when she had finished. "You play like a butcher. Don't ever play for me again."

Cherry gasped. "No, Mr. Scott. I'd be glad not to!"

Miss Kitty broke out laughing. "Don't feel hurt. My brother lives in and for music, and is a perfectionist besides. Awful!"

Scott Owens looked sheepish. "Perhaps you can sing?"

"I positively *can't* sing!" Cherry said in terror.

"Sing *Swanee* River," her patient commanded. "I'll accompany you. Stand there. Breathe, now."

He took Cherry's place at the first piano. His hands softly strummed out the opening bars, and the piano sang like a voice. Cherry added a few indifferent notes of her own. One of the poodles started to bark.

"No," he said sadly, "you can't sing. But," he looked up at her and that deep-down smile started all over again, "I like you very much just the same."

"Thank you," Cherry murmured. "I—I was watching your hands. On that magnificent piano." His hands were marvels of flexibility, strength, and control. They reminded her of surgeons' hands. The superb piano had been resonant and sensitive to his touch as if it were alive.

The musician looked pleased that she understood. "Go sit down and I'll play the waltz for you. Then later," his smile deepened, "you can revenge yourself by nursing me."

On a divan Miss Kitty whispered to her, "You were a brave girl. Scott rarely plays for anybody. That's a compliment. He likes you. Ssh, now."

They paid him the courtesy of not talking but listening while he played. Cherry realized gradually that he played the Chopin waltz again, not to embarrass her, not even to teach her for he was not concerned with teaching, but to clear her jangled, faulty, tormenting notes out of his oversensitive hearing. Now it was loveliness come to life in the air.

Upstairs in her enormous new room, Cherry gathered together her impressions. How inconsistent Scott Owens was—timid yet tyrannical, withdrawn and oversensitive but with a sense of humor, tactless and yet kindness itself, physically frail but summoning up the considerable stamina of body and mind which his work demanded of him. The whole clue to him, she guessed, was his devotion and drive to music. Cherry understood

DO, RE, MI AND COMPANY

he was a very special person, not to be judged by usual standards. How could she be a good nurse to such a person?

Miss Kitty rapped and came in then, and talked to Cherry about this very thing.

"You know Scott is a cardiac case," she said, settling her large frame into a large chair by the open windows. "But his heart condition bothers him less than the kind of temperament he is both cursed and blessed with."

Earnestly she spoke for her brother, explaining, pleading for him, guarding him. Scott Owens had a highly keyed set of nerves, and painfully acute hearing. He reacted about ten times as intensely as a normal person to sounds and—unfortunately—to all experience. He was like an oversensitive instrument out of which the smallest incident drew a terrific response. Out of this extreme sensitivity, out of this boiling imagination, his music was created. It was the price of his great gift and joy in music.

"He really suffers," his sister said. "It isn't pretended temperament, and it isn't lack of self-control, for he tries not to take things so hard. But small things which you or I would throw off can upset him for days. If he receives a discouraging notice from a critic, or has a tussle with a new composition, he may get too emotionally 'paralyzed' to work. Or he may even become physically ill. I know where those heart attacks come from—from emotional upsets."

"So we have to protect him all we can. I see."

"Yes. Keep him as quiet and calm as possible. Keep him out of crowds or big parties, away from any excessive excitement. Don't let autograph seekers and telephone pests annoy him. No noise, above all! Be easygoing and humorous ourselves. He's almost totally impractical. Knows nothing of business or money matters. He knows very little except music. I often wish—" Miss Owens sighed and changed her mind.

"I wish too we didn't have to travel so much on concert tour. Scott's so intense and impressionable that he soaks up travel impressions avidly and it wears him out."

"But his *American Landscape Suite* must have been written out of travel impressions," Cherry said.

"Yes. That's how he functions. Can you imagine him in money dealings? But what really worries me—" She frowned and turned her head away from the strong light at the window. Cherry could not see Miss Kitty's shadowed face, only the reddish hair. "What really worries me is what would happen to Scott if a real and big trouble hit him. I'm afraid his heart might— I try to take care of all practical things for him, yet— See here, Miss Cherry. Never—"

Cherry waited in the waning daylight. Now Miss Owens turned her face and Cherry could see the same panicky expression she had seen that day in Bluewater and again that very afternoon.

DO, RE, MI AND COMPANY 55

"Never mention Uncle Matthew in front of Scott. If anyone does, change the subject as fast as you can."

"But at the séance—you—?"

Miss Kitty forced a laugh. "Oh, I adore all fortunetellers. It's only a harmless amusement. Forget that Mrs. Crawford, why don't you? Forget the whole afternoon! I'm going to a better reader quite soon, you and Scott shall come along. It's fun. This man has the most picturesque studio—"

She rattled along about unimportant details. Cherry's attention was not sidetracked. It troubled her that the mere mention of an unexplained Uncle Matthew could throw her patient into a dangerous state. And Miss Kitty—so persistent, so anxious almost, in seeking out seers—She must be troubled, too, and seeking answers. What had gone wrong in this house?

Miss Owens was talking now about Cherry's work here and Cherry had to pay attention. "We don't expect you to wear a uniform or keep fixed hours, for resident nursing like this on a chronic case. Of course you'll be on emergency call day and night, but we'll manage four free hours every day for you. We want you to be like a member of the family—"

Cherry inquired tactfully about meals, about family visitors. A nurse was an outsider from the family circle, after all.

"Why, the idea! You'll take your meals with us and when we have visitors, we certainly want you there too.

That reminds me! A few close friends are dropping in for supper this evening."

Cherry murmured her thanks. She was genuinely grateful. She suspected how lonely a nurse's lot could be, in a less friendly household than this one.

"You won't wear a uniform," Miss Kitty rushed on, "that is, unless Scott has an attack and you have to do some actual nursing. And oh, yes, please watch out for the furniture. A lot of pieces are antiques and I'd hate to have medicine splashed on it, or a mark left from a hot-water bottle. Another thing. You'll have to keep your eye on my brother to suit *his* schedule. He works very hard and won't stand for interruptions. *Please* don't be one of those officious nurses who flurries into a household, and is 'obliged' to rearrange and disrupt everything, and expects the whole family to wait on her, and keeps the place in an uproar!"

Cherry grinned and said there was not much danger of that. She asked when she could meet Scott Owens's doctor, to secure his orders for the patient.

"He'll be here for supper, too. Get dressed, now. Wear something pretty!" Miss Kitty flashed out of Cherry's room, then poked her head back in. "Don't tell Scott about this conversation. Don't ever let him know I mentioned Uncle Matthew."

"I promise."

Cherry puzzled over their talk as she showered and changed. Miss Kitty was a bit inconsistent too.

DO, RE, MI AND COMPANY 57

Practical, yet she sought out fortunetellers. Sensible as a pair of high shoes, yet rattlebrained. But on the whole, Cherry thought her a grand person and counted herself fortunate to be associated with two such up-and-doing, openhearted people. A third important person with whom she must succeed in her dealings was the unknown doctor. She wondered what he might be like, as she brushed out her coal-black curls and slipped into a cool white linen dress. She was fastening pearls around her throat when something leaped on her shoulder.

Cherry jumped. A small furry face looked questioningly into hers, tiny claws clung through her dress. It was Octave, the Persian.

"Hello, Octave," Cherry ventured.

"Meow," replied the cat, satisfied that he had been acknowledged and duly greeted. He proceeded to drape himself about Cherry's neck like a fur piece. He felt soft and very warm and heavy, particularly on a summer's evening, but such ecstatic purring should be respected. Cherry walked down the long flights of stairs, Octave clinging to her, and hoped the Owens's physician would figuratively leap to greet her too.

Do, Re, and Mi appeared first in the living room door, yapping with jealousy. Octave waved his plumed tail, lightly leaped down, strolled majestically through and past the poodles, climbed into one of the open grand pianos, and curled up for a nap on the sounding board. The three poodles stood around looking routed.

Next in the living-room doorway came Miss Owens, in green now, and with her a comfortable-looking, middle-aged man.

"There you are! This is Miss Cherry Ames. Dr. Pratt."

He and Cherry shook hands. Cherry liked him on sight: his bulk, his keen, honest, brown eyes, even the way his jacket carelessly fell open.

"Glad you're here, Miss Ames. You have a patient who's very precious to thousands of people. Drop in at my office any time tomorrow morning and we'll talk over ways for you to pester him." He chuckled.

"You can talk to her now, George, if you want to," Miss Kitty said. "Scott is upstairs and the others won't be here for a few minutes yet, and I must give Jen a hand."

"Sure, all right, Kate."

She left, and Dr. Pratt and Cherry sat down together.

"Well, now," he said, frankly looking Cherry over. "You're a little younger than I expected—But so much the better! You'll be cheerful company for Scott. I don't expect miracles of my nurses, anyhow—haven't any illusions about 'em." Cherry suspected he was joking in all seriousness.

"I'm a busy doctor, Miss Ames," he went on. "I'll give you my orders just once, and expect you to manage on that. But any time you're not sure, or need me, I'll do my utmost—or I should say, *we'll* do our utmost together for Scott, won't we?"

DO, RE, MI AND COMPANY

"We certainly will," Cherry nodded eagerly. "I'll work hard for you, Dr. Pratt."

"Good girl. You drop by in the morning, as I said. I want to discuss this case with you privately and in detail. Let's not ever talk too much here, where Scott might overhear and worry, mm? Whispering in the hall's no good, either. When he's sick, write any questions you may have on a slip of paper and hand it to me along with the chart." "Our secret system, Cherry."

They grinned at each other in friendly understanding. Cherry sent up a silent hurrah in favor of Dr. George Pratt.

They spent the next several moments in companionable silence while they waited for Miss Kitty to return. Soon, she entered the room carrying a big bowl of water which she set near the pianos, to supply needed moisture for the wood of their delicate sounding boards. Octave took a drink out of it. Jen, in a fresh white apron, followed with a tray full of silver and china and linens. Lucien, an elderly man with a completely happy, irresponsible air, lugged in a pile of folding chairs. No one spoke, simply worked. Cherry, after offering to help Miss Kitty and being refused, watched the preparations with interest.

Lucien pulled out four small tables from against the walls, placed them before the several divans, added folding chairs around them. Jen then set three of these tables for supper, and set up near by the fourth table, a long larger one, as a buffet. Presto, a dining room! Meanwhile, Miss Kitty was lighting dozens of candles. The two rooms glowed. A breeze stirred the curtains at the windows. From upstairs waves of music rippled from Scott Owens's piano.

Cherry was just deciding this was all highly romantic and Bohemian, when there was a crash at the front door. A voice boomed mournfully:

"I am starving from hunger! All day to eat I forget it! Now up the steps I fall down! Please!"

An enormously fat and funny man puffed into the room. Everybody laughed, they couldn't help it. Miss Owens gasped out:

"Bébé, did you hurt yourself?"

Bébé—or Baby—shook his large bald head. He caught sight of Cherry, and waddled over to her.

"Who is this beautiful?" He beamed at her. "I like your smell."

Cherry almost leaped off the couch. Dr. Pratt roared.

"Smell, no?" Bébé perspired earnestly. "Smill? Ah—I catch it—*smile*." He turned to Cherry and bowed from his rubber-tire waist. Then he enunciated laboriously, "I like your *smile*, no smell. Smell is with the nose? Ha, I think so."

Miss Owens came over, laughing. "Miss Cherry Ames, Mr. Franz Walter, the composer. Franz—Bébé—is Viennese. What he cannot say in English, he says superbly in music."

The fat man murmured acknowledgments and demanded if Scott had yet played through his, Franz's, new work for piano and orchestra.

"Already no, hah?" He waddled to the stairs and shouted. "Scott! Quick you should be down-coming!"

Scott yelled back some happy, indistinguishable insult. The doorbell tinkled. Lucien admitted a dignified elderly couple. Everyone rose to greet them.

"Dr. and Mrs. Richard White. I believe you know everyone, except Miss Ames here. Bertha, let me have your gloves and bag. So glad you felt well enough to come."

Cherry waited until the couple were seated and chatting with Bébé and the doctor. Then she sat down too, beside Miss Kitty. "Who are they?" she whispered. They were both very quiet: serious, gray-haired, rather formal. Mrs. White wore a long dark dinner frock.

"He's one of the best American conductors." Miss Owens named the symphony orchestra of this midwest city. "That's his orchestra. Mrs. White is a darling but terribly shy. You see how subdued they are? They lost their son, their only child, in the war."

Cherry looked at them sympathetically, looked away. Lucien passed apéritifs and canapés, on which Bébé pounced. Cherry was exploring the delights of icy tomato juice accompanied by salty red caviar, when the doorbell chimed again. Cherry realized that it played "Do, Re, Mi"—probably in honor of those ridiculous poodles. Then a tragically beautiful woman strode into the room.

She walked exactly like Octave as she moved among the friends, and she had the same brooding eyes. But where Octave was golden, she was stark black and white—hair brushed flat like black satin, and moon-white skin. All the people in the room crowded around this tall slender woman in her long gown, adoring her, somehow protecting her.

The hostess took Cherry by the arm. "Miss Carmela Wheeler, our new nurse and mentor, Miss Cherry Ames."

The woman looked at Cherry thoughtfully and said, "If I had ever had a daughter, perhaps she would have looked like you."

Cherry stammered a response. There was something electric in this woman's presence. A few moments later, in another part of the room, Cherry managed to ask Miss Owens about her.

"Contralto. Not opera. Song recitals. Scott writes for her. So does Bébé and every composer I know—they're all in love with her. Half Italian, half American."

"But that—that *look*? That almost tragic—?"

"It's a long story. Nobody really knows the whole story. Tell you about it sometime. Oh, here's our dinner!"

Jen sent up the first tray of food, they found places at the several small tables, and Lucien started to serve a chilled consommé. The supper was rather hectic.

DO, RE, MI AND COMPANY

"Move over!" Miss Kitty demanded and plopped down beside Cherry on the couch.

"I play now for the soup, I play!" Bébé boomed and rushed to the piano.

Scott came slowly down the stairs. Dr. Pratt shook his head at him: Scott should have used the small stairwell elevator provided for him. But Scott made a face at the doctor, drank his soup standing and in one gulp, and strode toward the second piano. He and Bébé playing together made the candles waver, china tremble, walls ring.

Lucien disappeared with emptied soup cups and reappeared with laden platters for the buffet table. The eight people milled around, serving themselves, sitting now at this table or that so they could visit. Miss Kitty announced loudly that she would tell their fortunes, whether they liked it or not. Dr. White and Dr. Pratt became two immovable figures frozen over a chess game. Talk swirled learnedly of music, books, politics, trade, people. The moon shone in through the windows. The beautiful Carmela sang.

It was the funniest, wackiest, most brilliant evening Cherry had ever lived through. It ended finally with the candles guttering, the guests crowding the door, and Bébé waving his arms and shouting in farewell:

"I have come to tell you that I am no longer here!"

CHAPTER IV

~~~~~~~~~~~~~~~~~~~~~~~~~~~~~~~~~~~~~

The Fortunetellers

THE DAY BEFORE THE THREE OF THEM WERE TO LEAVE on concert tour, Miss Kitty insisted they all go consult a fortuneteller. Her brother called it silly, Cherry protested as much as she could—but Miss Owens bundled them into the car and off they went.

"I made this appointment a week in advance," she sputtered. "This is my favorite reader! Usually Gregory Carroll won't see anyone without *two* weeks' advance appointment! He's taking us as a special favor, because I'm one of his best clients—I rely on him for everything—that is, since I've known him. I found out about him only just before we left for Bluewater. He's marvelous. Today's sitting really is a special favor to me—he's awfully sought after and busy."

"As a special favor to you," Scott Owens grunted, "for a big, fat fee."

THE FORTUNETELLERS 65

And Cherry wondered why a fortuneteller, of all people, insisted on advance appointments.

They drove to a residential hotel in one of the most expensive sections of the city, and went up to the Carroll suite. There were no mystic trappings here, only large, beautifully furnished rooms: Chippendale chairs, paintings and prints, walls lined with books. It looked to Cherry like a movie set of what a rich gentleman's apartment should be, ultracorrect, too perfect, too studied, not quite genuine. Or perhaps, Cherry thought, she was overly suspicious.

The Owens party was admitted by an elderly man who seemed to know Miss Kitty. He was a dried-up, drab little man, in spectacles and a dust-colored jacket such as librarians wear. His air was precise and pedantic. Cherry suspected he was stuffed with sawdust. He seemed to be a sort of employee or upper servant.

"Please come in. I am Mr. Thatch, the secretary." His voice was humdrum, but he was trying to be amiable. "Please sit down. Mr. Carroll is occupied on the telephone. May I offer you coffee while you are waiting?"

They took seats around the handsome room and Mr. Thatch fussed about, pouring coffee for them. He set the silver pot back on his neatly littered desk.

"I must apologize for the appearance of my desk. We have so much work to do. I tell Mr. Carroll that if he accepts any more clients, he will have a nervous breakdown." He noticed Scott's and Cherry's disdainful looks. "You don't believe we work hard, sir? You don't give credence to prognostication? Neither do many people until they have met Gregory Carroll. Please forgive me for pressing the point, but he is extraordinary—beyond explanation—I venture to say you will find him strangely gifted."

Cherry sipped her coffee and wondered. The secretary chatted obediently with Miss Owens of trivia. Scott Owens's attention wandered to a fine harpsichord that stood along the wall.

"Let me open it for you," Mr. Thatch offered. He walked stiffly to the antique piano. "Would you care to try it, sir? We keep it in tune, to preserve it—you see the construction?" he said with a professor's air. "The upper octave is shrill but on the whole, the tone is acceptable."

Cherry saw how quickly the musician was disarmed of his suspicions, by this talk of music. Clever of Mr. Thatch. He seemed to know a great deal about music, antiques, many things—he seemed to be a highly educated, if a tiresome, man.

An inner door opened and a man of about forty-five stood there. Gregory Carroll was striking for his grave and spiritual look. Small-boned, intensely quiet, with a taut cameo face, he might have been an early friar. Or an artist listening with an almost religious dedication to the inner voices of beauty. He might have been

THE FORTUNETELLERS

wearing simple robes instead of his dark blue business suit.

He smiled at Miss Owens. "You look much happier today, Miss Kitty. Mr. Owens"—they shook hands "—I hope I can be of service to you. And Miss—?"

"Miss Cherry Ames," Mr. Thatch presented her. "Mr. Owens's nurse."

Gregory Carroll turned on her eyes of a cold blue that seemed to be both transparent and full of light. They were extraordinary eyes. "Miss Ames. How do you do. Will you wait here, please?" He ushered the Owenses into the next room and shut the door.

Mr. Thatch puttered around refilling Cherry's cup. He sat down, prim and dutiful, to entertain her. "Have you known the Owenses long, Miss Ames?"

"Not very long."

"Oh.—Mr. Owens is quite ill, isn't he? Angina pectoris, I believe his sister said. What a pity. A man in that condition should be protected from worries. I presume that is part of your duties as his nurse."

"Yes. Er—good coffee."

"Thank you. You would know if anything is worrying him? Or if Miss Kitty is worrying?"

"That's right," said Cherry.

Mr. Thatch gingerly sipped his coffee. "I often wonder what a celebrity's past must be like. A man like Mr. Owens must have made a long, difficult climb to fame. I do admire such a man."

Cherry said in some exasperation, "I haven't known Mr. Owens long enough to know anything about his past."

Mr. Thatch coughed and was silent. He patted his lips with his pocket handkerchief. Then, hesitatingly, he said:

"As the Owenses' nurse, may I confide to you something which troubles me? Miss Kitty is such an enthusiast for fortunetelling that I am concerned about her. It has occurred to me that she might fall into some charlatan's hands sometime. Mr. Carroll is honest and can be of service to her. But some of these others"—he picked at one neat trouser knee—"the others might accept her money, suggest worrisome ideas to her, and do her and her brother real harm. That is why I asked you, a moment ago, if either of them is worrying about anything."

The elderly man looked at Cherry earnestly. Then he rose and rapped on the door and inquired about sending a cable. Gregory Carroll gave instructions and called, "Miss Ames, don't you want to come in now, too?"

Cherry went into a smaller room dominated by Gregory Carroll seated at a vast desk. She sat down beside Scott Owens who said with a grin, "I need another nonbeliever for moral support. They're telling my fortune in spite of my protests."

Gregory Carroll smiled. Miss Owens's rapt expression did not change.

THE FORTUNETELLERS 69

"I can tell you this," Gregory Carroll said softly. "The influences now are almost all good. But long ago, you had a terrible experience."

Scott Owens trembled. He got out, "Who hasn't had a bad experience at one time or another?"

"A terrible and unjust experience," Carroll pursued. "Most unjust. It lasted about—let's see—your ordeal lasted about two years."

Scott Owens suddenly turned gray. Cherry was alarmed for her patient. Two years of *what?*

"But that is all over," Carroll gently went on, "and the indications for the future are encouraging. For the immediate future, great personal success—through your work—"

"My brother always gets excellent notices on all his concerts!"

Scott said crossly, "For heaven's sake, don't put the words in his mouth! Who's telling this prediction, Kit, you or Mr. Carroll?"

Gregory Carroll said, "An illness is coming. Perhaps caused by worry."

Cherry did not like this suggestion to her patient that he would fall ill. Miss Kitty asked sharply, "What would my brother have to worry about?"

The reader slowly shook his head. "Something returning from the past. I'd prefer to draw up a more detailed chart and really study the matter before saying exactly what. I don't mean to alarm you. I merely want to warn you."

"I suppose there's an extra charge for this chart?" The musician made it not a question but a sarcastic statement.

"It's a good deal of work," Miss Kitty retorted. "If there is something in the prognostications to be alarmed about, I want to know exactly what it is!"

Gregory Carroll nodded, and turned to Cherry.

"And you, young lady. Don't meddle in others' affairs. You won't help them—you will only bring trouble, for them and for yourself. Aside from that, you can be a good influence for Mr. Owens. Your vibrations are sympathetic to his."

"I expect my nursing techniques will do him more practical good than my 'vibrations,' Mr. Carroll."

The musician said shortly, "This has been very interesting and now I have to leave. If you'll excuse us, sir—"

"But, Scott," his sister said, "we aren't finished—"

Scott Owens stood up. The reader rose too, and held out his hand.

"Good-bye, Mr. Owens, and thank you for coming. Watch your health and especially watch out for the past returning. Good-bye, Miss Kitty ... Miss Ames. Perhaps next time I will be able to tell you something of a happier nature. But whatever it is, I will tell you only the truth."

THE FORTUNETELLERS 71

Mr. Thatch showed them out. All the way downstairs, all during the drive home, Scott Owens muttered his annoyance at "this impertinent nonsense." He had not wanted his fortune told; Kitty had teased him until he had to accede. Only his sister's remark, "He said *two years,* Scott"—only that silenced him. Cherry was very curious indeed. She did not want or intend to pry into her patient's personal affairs. But it was part of her work to safeguard him against upsetting things, and she was alarmed now at how gray and tired he seemed, after what had been said. She would call Dr. Pratt at once.

Jen took one look at him and groaned.

"Mr. Scott looks like a string! You'll never be able to get him on a train tomorrow! Miss Kitty, haven't you better sense than to pester him this way?"

Cherry telephoned Dr. Pratt. On his instructions, she spent the rest of that day making the pianist take nourishment at short intervals, practice only three hours instead of his accustomed five, and lie down. His sister did everybody's packing, sent last-minute telegrams to concert-hall managers en route, and keep Bébé and other callers from going upstairs. Scott complained that they all treated him like "the Koh-I-Noor diamond, only breakable." Cherry replied that he was pretty valuable, at that, "and besides we like you!" She refrained from repeating what Dr. Pratt had impressed on her: in angina pectoris, any one heart attack can prove fatal.

72   *CHERRY AMES, PRIVATE DUTY NURSE*

They started out lightheartedly enough next morning. Cherry of course took her instrument kit, medicines, and uniform with her, but wore street clothes. Although the first leg of their journey was to be only half a day, Miss Owens had taken a private drawing room on the train, so Scott could practice.

"Practice?" Cherry said in astonishment. "In here?" The three of them were crowded into a small Pullman room, door closed, rocking with the motion of the speeding train. It felt a little like playing house on rails. "A piano in here?"

"Why, certainly," the musician said merrily. He seemed to have put out of his mind all of yesterday's nonsense. "Kit, where did you stow *Dr. Gradus Ad Parnassum?*"

"Right here." Miss Kitty produced a book of music scores and a strange-looking, boxlike contraption, which she opened and set on a Pullman table before the train seat. It was a portable, mute keyboard for practice purposes. Scott Owens sat down to it, ran his hands over the silent keyboard several times to limber up his fingers. Then he played, beating time with his foot, earnestly nodding his head, hands and wrists flying in many technical flourishes—and not a sound came out! It was so ludicrous that Cherry got to giggling, and finally laughed out loud.

Scott Owens looked at her, solemn as an owl. "If I don't practice for one day, I notice it. If I don't practice

THE FORTUNETELLERS 73

for two days, my friends notice it. If I don't practice for three days, my audiences notice it. Now quiet, please. Don't interrupt my music."

And he fell to thumping the keyboard again with all his might—and achieving only a few wooden grunts. Cherry wiped the tears of laughter out of her eyes. She managed to keep a straight face for the rest of the journey only by following Miss Kitty's example and reading.

By afternoon they were off the train and established comfortably in a hotel in a small city. Miss Kitty had wanted to break the journey for her brother, having him sleep overnight in a hotel bed rather than in a train berth. Cherry insisted that the pianist have additional milk and sandwiches—for he was anemic and anemia intensified his cardiac difficulty. As he was finishing his milk, in their hotel suite, Miss Kitty admitted she had a second reason for stopping over in this town. There was a fortuneteller she wanted to visit.

"No, no, not that!" Her brother's thin frame shook with laughter. "Kit, I'm ashamed of you!"

"But this one's supposed to be a real witch! Way out in the country. You can stay here—you can rest—or practice—"

"Nothing doing! You know how I detest hotel rooms."

Cherry spoke up, trying to sound professional. "Mr. Scott, you have the big task of a concert ahead of you. You really should keep quiet."

"Be reasonable, Scott. I won't go either."

"Oh, you'll go anyway. I know you! No. I'll go along—to keep you from telling all the family secrets."

The hotel quickly secured a car and driver for them. They drove through the town, and set off along a state highway.

The car did not stay on the highway for more than a few miles. It swung off onto side roads. No more villages appeared. Then they drove off the asphalt and hit dirt roads, leading to lonely farms. The driver complained that he did not know where he was going. But Miss Owens called out "Keep going!" and gave directions. The car jolted along mere lanes now and wound up in a tangle of underbrush. They stopped, unable to go further. The silence was profound, until their ears picked up the hum of insects, the snapping of a twig.

"This can't be it!"

"This is it. We'll get out and walk."

They pushed their way through branches, following a rut in the earth. Cherry thought she heard a telephone ring somewhere. But she must have imagined it, she decided, for when they abruptly emerged into a clearing, there was only a tumble-down shack and a half-ruined barn.

Chickens ran around the house and filth lay everywhere. The driver snorted and went back to wait in the car. Miss Kitty boldly marched through rusted cans, rainsoaked boards, burned cornstalks, up to the shack.

THE FORTUNETELLERS

Scott followed laughing, and Cherry, tossing back her black curls, felt relieved that her patient regarded this as only a lark.

"Is anybody here? Hoo-hoo!"

Miss Kitty's echo quavered back at her.

"Hello!" called Scott. "Come down off your broomstick and brew us a potion of snakes' tongues!" He coughed then from the exertion of shouting.

Out of a broken window peered a hag of a woman. Her loose mouth, even the stringy hair about her face, was stained yellow with chewing tobacco.

"Who're ye? Git away!"

"We've come to ask you to read cards for us," Miss Kitty called, unperturbed.

"Ain't readin' today. Git along!" The sloven spat from the window.

Miss Owens argued and cajoled. She offered good payment. She named the woman friend who had sent her.

"Wal. I reckon I kin read fur ye. Go 'long in."

Scott whispered to Cherry, "She looks like a caution for cats."

Cherry whispered back, "And just look at this hovel. I wish I had a pail full of disinfectant."

This was the worst poverty Cherry had ever seen. The cabin room had a dirt floor, no windows, a roof with a hole gaping toward the sky. A few broken stools, a box, a rusty coal stove, and an old table showed in the shadows. The stench was awful. They shooed chickens off the stools and gingerly sat down.

They waited for long minutes. Nearly ten minutes. Two people were talking in the next room, but Cherry could not hear what they said.

The hag shuffled in. Close up, Cherry saw she was barefoot, not as old as she appeared at first, and had an inexpressibly stupid and malevolent face. Suddenly Cherry wanted to get out of here. This whole situation was unhealthy. But she could not catch Scott's eye, to signal him, and Miss Kitty seemed to be enjoying herself.

"I understand you live here alone?" she questioned the woman. "My friend says you have supernatural powers. A sort of nature seer?"

"Live here with my old man. Lyin' sick, he is." The hag snapped, "Lay out yer money on the table afore I read."

Miss Kitty counted out bills. The woman watched, seemed satisfied. Then she sat down before the table and thumbed through a deck of greasy cards. These she lay out in three semicircles. She pored over them, chewing her wad of tobacco. Then she lifted her head.

"Yer name ain't what ye pretend it is!" She looked directly at Scott. "Mind now, I don't know yer name—neither of yer names. The cards here—*they say it.*"

"I don't want my fortune told," Scott said.

"Silly!" Miss Kitty laughed. "Try it, be a sport!"

THE FORTUNETELLERS 77

"But I kin find out yer name—both of 'em." The hag persisted slyly.

"Tell somebody else's fortune," Scott said, less steadily.

"There's papers about yer names. And they're at"—the woman hesitated for a long time—"in a box, mebbe." She never took her eyes from the man. He changed color. The hag nodded. "Yep. In a box. In a good safe box, hey?"

Miss Kitty, who seemed to notice the threatening undertone, said evenly, "You're making a mountain out of a molehill. People often alter their names for professional reasons. As a matter of fact, this man with me—"

"The box, the box," the hag muttered. Again her stupid eyes fastened on Scott. "You better watch that box. The cards say the box is in—" Again that long, probing pause. Cherry felt a shiver spread up her spine. "—the box is in—"

The woman grinned evilly at Scott Owens. He had turned ashen and was beginning to sweat.

"That's enough!" Cherry shouted. She sprang to her feet, seized her patient by the arm, and dragged him out into the open air. He swayed with weakness. Cherry was thoroughly alarmed and angry. "Get that car if you can!" Cherry yelled to Miss Kitty. "How can you submit Mr. Scott to this!"

Frightened, the sister ran out. Together she and Cherry half lifted, half walked the frail man back to the car. The slovenly woman lounged in her doorway, speculatively watching them.

Later, after they had gotten Scott safely back to the hotel and into bed, with the danger of attack averted, Cherry apologized to her employer. She emphasized how important peace of mind was to the ill man. She reminded Miss Kitty that fright or anger or emotional shock could bring on an attack.

Miss Owens knew all this. She truly wanted to take good care of her brother. Yet now, with rest having made Scott comfortable and calm again, the fright seemed to her unnecessary. She lightly laughed off Cherry's warning.

"Of course I'm not angry with you for shouting at me, my dear. You're absolutely right. But aren't you taking all these little fortunetelling jaunts much too seriously? Why, your attitude persuades Scott to take them overseriously, too. Don't wear such a long face about such a little thing!"

Cherry was unable to convince her that, with her "little jaunts," she was being very foolish. Dangerously foolish.

Nor did Miss Owens explain to Cherry whether or not her brother had taken a professional name. However, that was none of the nurse's business.

But the nurse began to wonder. Was there some mystery surrounding Scott Owens? He lived in a blaze of public notice, like all celebrities. Did something

THE FORTUNETELLERS 79

ominous or unhappy lie buried in his past? Something involving two years of his life. Something which could return and whose return he dreaded. And now this matter—related? unrelated?—of possibly having taken another name. And where did an Uncle Matthew fit in?

"I'll stick to my nursing job and stop speculating," Cherry promised herself. "Only I wish my bump of curiosity weren't such a great, big, lively bump!"

They traveled by train again and came to a large southwestern city. Here Scott was to give the first of five concerts scheduled for five various towns. Miss Kitty had arranged their arrival a full day and a half ahead of the concert, so her brother could rest. Besides, he would have to see newspaper reporters, try out the piano provided for him, and probably attend a party which the local musical circles usually tendered him.

But Cherry was waiting for Miss Kitty to say, sooner or later—and she did say, at breakfast in the hotel on the second day:

"Now, Scott, don't be angry, but there's a woman here in town whom I simply have to see. This morning."

"A fortuneteller?" her brother inquired dryly.

"Well—Yes."

Cherry shook her head at Miss Owens. Her black eyes burned in warning, and her cheeks flamed redder than usual.

"Of course I'll go alone," Miss Owens said hastily. "I'll just—"

"You'll go alone, and just be played for a complete sucker! Oh, yes, Kit, that will be fine. Just fine. You'll let some unscrupulous charlatan drag all our innermost secrets out of you—you'll compromise my good reputation—you'll just ruin—"

"Please!" Cherry interrupted. She was intensely embarrassed to have the Owenses quarrel and discuss before her matters she had no right to know. "Please, Mr. Scott. You must not excite yourself. If Dr. Pratt were here, he'd be horrified. Right before a concert is no time of all times to wear yourself out."

"That's right." Miss Kitty leaned forward anxiously. "Let's drop the whole subject. I won't go see this woman. Is that better, Scott?"

His thin face remained tense. "I know what you'll do. You'll go anyway. No. I won't let you out of my sight. This thing can be dangerous, I tell you—"

"Scott, don't work yourself up!"

"I'll tell you what we'll do!" He was trembling, nearly shouting in his excitement and worry. "All right, we'll go to that fortuneteller! I'll go along to see that you—that you don't—"

Cherry said sharply, "Mr. Scott, pull yourself together."

He calmed as suddenly as if she had slapped him out of hysteria.

"You're right, Miss Cherry. It's nothing but a racket. I don't take it seriously. If only Kit weren't such a fool."

THE FORTUNETELLERS

"We'll tell the fortuneteller's fortune, by gum! We'll scare the spots off her phony cards!" It was a weak joke but Cherry made it, and made herself laugh. Scott Owens laughed a little, too. Then his sister joined in, and the tension was gone.

Cherry was somewhat reassured when she saw the quiet house and the quiet, genteel, little person whom they had come to see.

Miss Pride might have been some struggling, respectable seamstress. In fact, there was a sign "Sewing" in her window, and a sewing machine piled with materials. There was poverty in this house, too, with its threadbare carpets and shabby, scrupulously clean furniture. Miss Pride herself had a spinster's neatness and primness. She ushered them into her parlor, took the faded cretonne cover off the bird cage so they could see her canary, and asked if they thought it wasn't very warm today. It all seemed ordinary enough, drab and musty and pitiful. The whole house looked and smelled as if it had died. Little Miss Pride sat in the midst of her few belongings like a forlorn traveler coming from and going to nowhere.

"What would you like to know?" she asked timidly. "No, I don't read cards. I just—see."

"Well, what do you see?" Scott Owens challenged.

Miss Pride folded her hands in her lap and gazed at them. Miss Owens scribbled a note to Cherry. *Mr. Thatch told me she's one of those rare people who are really psychic.*

The little seamstress said hesitantly, "You seem to have two lives. I don't know exactly how to describe it. I see you in another life under another name. Two lives and—and two names, I think."

Miss Kitty stiffened but held her tongue.

Scott grumbled, "Why don't you fakers ever tell something about the future? Always the past, the past. Anyone can predict what already has happened."

Miss Pride drew a long, shaky breath. "All right, sir. You are facing an illness. I don't like to tell people bad things. But if you insist—Well—You are facing some trouble, coming out of the past. That seems to be what brings on the illness. Excuse me, sir, but I do see it."

This was so possible in Scott's condition, and so exactly what Gregory Carroll had predicted, that all three callers were shaken.

Miss Pride said suddenly, "You had trouble about money, and an uncle." Scott started, restrained himself.

Now Miss Pride's expression changed, so subtly that Cherry could not define her strained look.

"About the two names. Haven't you some papers of proof about that, somewhere?"

Miss Kitty nodded her red head before Scott could stop her. Her brother glared at her.

"Well, never mind, no matter," Miss Pride said breathlessly. "About you, ma'am." She turned her pinched face to Miss Kitty, and now the strain had gone out of it. "You're going traveling. Just a short trip

THE FORTUNETELLERS

for now, and probably several short trips later. Business, it seems to be." She talked on vaguely. Scott Owens cut her short.

"You're rambling. You're not telling a thing."

The little seamstress colored. "I can tell the young lady here"—she looked at Cherry—"that she ought not to go out looking for trouble. If she does, she'll find it. Bad trouble."

Cherry was amazed. It was true that she was tantalized to unravel the mystery clouding Scott Owens.

Miss Pride said almost pleadingly, "Don't interfere in anything that doesn't concern you, young lady."

"Stuff and nonsense!" Scott exclaimed, getting to his feet. "What are you trying to keep her from learning or doing? What are you trying to find out from us?"

In the crestfallen silence, the canary sang.

Miss Pride defenselessly accepted what Scott chose to pay her, and took them to the door.

"Good-bye. Please don't be angry with me," she whispered. "Be—be careful." Then she added something very strange. "I can't help myself. Good-bye."

She shut the door. Cherry thought she heard Miss Pride sobbing, on the other side of the closed door.

CHAPTER V

On Tour

CHERRY NEVER BEFORE HAD BEEN BACKSTAGE. WHAT she saw there before, during, and after Scott Owens's concert, impressed her as fantastic. It was, besides, a terrific ordeal for her patient.

Around noon on the day of the concert—the concert was scheduled for evening—Scott began to "agonize," as his sister called it. He paced their hotel sitting room, sat down and played fiercely on the rented piano, ranged the room once more, held his head, wrung his hands.

"I'll never get through this concert! Never! Never!"

"You always get through them, Scott."

"But not this time! I haven't whipped the Haydn into the shape I want—I'm not at all satisfied that the Shostakovitch is ready, I shouldn't have programmed it until next winter—Oh, ye gods! I wish I were home in bed!"

Cherry suffered right along with her patient. These hours of waiting for evening were nerve-racking. Facing several hundred critical people and performing for them, all alone, would be no joke, either.

Scott Owens had a nosebleed. Cherry stanched it as fast as she could, with medicated cotton, ice, lemon juice to drink. "Nerves," Miss Kitty said coolly. "He always has nosebleeds before a concert."

"But he's anemic, he can't afford to lose blood," Cherry worried. "We'd better feed him all he will take."

The unhappy musician refused to eat. "I've lost my appetite, honestly I have," he pleaded. Cherry could well believe him.

"A little milk, then, Mr. Scott."

He drank it obediently, and immediately threw it up. "As usual," Miss Kitty commented. Pacing the room, playing, lying down, rereading the music scores and marking them still again—the artist was in torture.

"Look how my fingers are trembling," he said and held them out before him. "I'll make all kinds of mistakes!"

"You'll do what you always tell others to do," his sister reassured him. "Press hard on the keys. That will stop the trembling. Pretend your ten fingers are ten hammers. Don't worry, Scott, press hard and your firm touch will return."

Cherry marveled at Miss Owens's calm. But later in the afternoon, she found the sister lying down in her own hotel room, with a wet towel over her eyes.

"Can you give me anything for a raging headache? Lord, no, Cherry, I'm not cool and collected! I'm nearly as upset as Scott is, but I don't dare let him see it! Do you know what depends on a single concert? His whole career! This tests his whole lifework! One bad concert and the critics pounce. Slipping, they'll say. Then Scott would feel so hurt that he'd really slip. Oh, pray, Cherry, pray. Scott has a very difficult program tonight."

"He won't let me give him any sedatives or even any simple treatments," Cherry murmured, as she tended Miss Kitty. "Tell me. Does Mr. Scott ever get a heart attack before or after a concert?"

"No, thank heavens, that's never happened yet."

Cherry sighed in relief. She knew that the typical attack of this cardiac condition started with a pain in the left shoulder, spread down the arm to the elbow, into the wrist, and even to the fingers. Mr. Scott could not play if agonizing pain struck his shoulder and arm and hand. Worse, any handicap, even temporary, to the musician's priceless arms and hands could throw him into panic. From panic and worry into attack, a vicious circle—

ON TOUR

"You see, Cherry, all this torment that Scott is going through isn't so bad for him, at that. It's perfectly natural; almost all musicians and many actors suffer like this before important performances. Scott sweats all the stage fright out of his system ahead of time. Then when he faces the audience, he's calm—still scared to death but reasonably calm. You'll see."

Miss Kitty was right. By evening, the artist was worn out but in quiet control of himself. Cherry was concerned that he looked so exhausted. "He'll get his second wind," his sister promised. "The minute he starts playing, he'll be fine."

The three of them drove to the concert hall three quarters of an hour before curtain time. They were all resplendent in summer evening dress. Managers, stagehands, a piano tuner, all appeared, wanting to speak to Scott. Miss Owens shooed them away from her brother.

"I'll see to the placing of the piano and the lights myself," she said. "He's already tried out the piano, thank you, and it's satisfactory." She went off with the backstage crew.

The musician and Cherry retired to the Green Room "—where the performers turn green with stage fright," Scott Owens joked. It was a perfectly quiet sitting room, dimly lighted. The artist put aside his scores, sat down, and closed his eyes. Cherry did not even stir. He seemed to be thinking, relaxing, summoning up his powers for the concentrated effort soon to come.

After a while, with Cherry, he left the Green Room and they peered out from the wings at the arriving audience. The house twinkled with hundreds of lights and was filled to the rafters. A smiling face, a sharp yellow dress, a man's white hair, someone's glinting jewel, sprang out at them from the moving sea of faces. Scott was elated. Still, his hands were ice cold and he was sweating. Cherry held tight to the stimulants she carried in her silk purse for him.

The magic moment arrived. The house lights dimmed. The audience quieted to a murmur. The manager brought chairs for Miss Kitty and Cherry to sit in the wings. Scott, Miss Kitty, Cherry stood looking out at the empty, brilliantly illumined stage. The gleaming dark piano stood open. The ivory keys shone.

"Luck, Scott!" His sister kissed him. She wiped his hands with her handkerchief. He patted her on the shoulder. Cherry's black eyes glowed good wishes at him.

He strode out alone and crossed the empty stage. He looked very tall and remote out there in the spotlight. Cherry with Miss Kitty heard the wave of applause, saw Scott bow, then the rustling silence. Scott sat down before the piano with his back to the wings and meditated a second before the keys. There was an expectant hush. Then the first firm notes pealed out.

He played magnificently—purer than Cherry had heard him on the radio, a shade less profound than when he played in the solitude of his upstairs study. But it was a superb, a bravura performance. The applause between numbers was thunderous. At intermission, Scott came staggering back in a triumphant daze and bolted into the Green Room. Cherry brought him a glass of water. Miss Kitty stood guard inside the door.

"How is it?" he asked his sister anxiously.

"You were never better. Just don't look at their faces. When you bow, look at the back wall. Don't forget to look up, though, at the balcony and boxes."

"Yes, Kit," he said like a little boy. "How are the acoustics?"

They did not talk much. Cherry said nothing at all. She made a close visual check and was satisfied that the musician felt well. Indeed, the performance, so long dreaded and prepared for, seemed to release and relax him. He went back on stage to play the second half of his program.

In this half were the more difficult numbers, including one of Bébé's which this audience had never heard before and might not like, at least not at first hearing. Scott Owens was nervous for his own and his friend's sake. Cherry admired his courage, for audiences can hiss and boo. She admired his generosity, too, in giving a fellow musician's composition a launching and the prestige of his own performance.

When Scott returned to the wings, the program completed, the audience roaring applause and bravos,

Cherry's patient was exhausted. He was drenched with perspiration. Still the audience clamored.

"Encore! Encore!" They left their seats and surged down the aisles and packed themselves around the stage. "Owens! Bravo! Encore!"

Scott went out to the close-packed ring of faces at his feet. Silence fell. Cherry heard him say, "Thank you. An encore."

Someone called out, "Play your own étude, Opus 1!"

Scott modestly shook his head at them, and sat down and played a brief Chopin waltz, the one he had played for Cherry. One, two, three short encores he played. Still his audience would not let him go, crying and applauding for more.

"Scott!" Miss Kitty hissed from the wings. "Come back here!"

He bowed apologetically to the upturned faces at the footlights and came back to his sister and Cherry in the wings.

"That's enough!" Miss Kitty whispered. "Don't make them sick of you. Always leave them wanting more."

Now the frail man really seemed exhausted and Cherry began to worry in earnest. His face was drained of color, his whole slight body sagged, his hands, veined with exertion, curled now like withered leaves. But the manager was summoning them, many voices and footsteps echoed behind them.

ON TOUR

Scott said wearily, "There's still the reception to be got through. I'm so tired."

For an hour longer, he stood backstage, with his fiercely protective sister beside him, while admirers shook his hand and chatted. Each person jealously tried to chat with the celebrated pianist a little longer than his neighbor chatted. Scott looked ready to drop but smiled and smiled, and said something appropriate to each one.

"He's got to go home now," Cherry frowned at Miss Kitty.

They got him out of the crowd and back to the hotel. He refused to go to bed. He had to wait just a little longer, he pleaded, for the one A.M. editions of tomorrow's newspapers. These would carry reviews of his concert.

The notices were excellent. Scott ate, smiled, and slept. Miss Kitty had "a good cry." Cherry put her stimulants back in the kit. It was all over.

But Cherry had spotted a symptom this evening which gravely disturbed her. It was the way the musician's left shoulder and arm had hung after the concert, as if in pain. If he *had* suffered pain, he was too dazed by that time, too exhausted and numbed, to pay attention to it. That arm was a danger signal. A signal to Cherry's trained eyes of impending heart attack.

It was two-thirty in the morning when Cherry secretly slipped downstairs to the hotel lobby. From a phone booth she telephoned Dr. Pratt long-distance.

The doctor's voice came distantly. "I don't believe the concert did this to him. Playing and concerts agree with him. What else has happened? What was there to worry him?"

"Fortunetellers—?"

"What nonsense is this?" asked the doctor after a pause.

"Nothing, really," Cherry replied quickly. "I'm sure he will be all right in the morning."

Yes, the concert was all over. Now, next day, it was all to do over again, in the next town. They packed and prepared to board another train.

At the railroad station, there were no drawing rooms to be had on their train. Miss Kitty was annoyed. She rushed around from ticket windows to passenger agent's office, hat bobbing militantly atop her reddish hair.

"Never mind," the pianist told her cheerfully. "I feel so well today that I don't need to be wrapped in cotton wool and hidden in any drawing room. Ah, with that concert behind me, I feel wonderful!"

Cherry grinned at her patient. "More fun anyway to sit in the regular car and see all the other passengers, isn't it?"

So they settled down in Pullman seats and Scott proceeded to amuse, amaze, and startle the passengers all around them by banging away at his silent keyboard.

Presently the three of them fell to talking about fortunetellers. Cherry noticed that the man across the aisle seemed to prick up his ears. But people bored by long trips often idly listen in on neighbors' conversation, and besides the man went on reading his magazine.

"I'll tell you what I think about these so-called fortune-tellers," Scott said. He was bright and lively today. "No, Kit, I'm not angry any more. But I've sworn off them, and I wish you would too."

"They've told us a lot of things," his sister bridled.

"Only things in the past."

"But accurate, even on family secrets."

"Want to know how they do it?" Scott asked derisively. "They haven't any second sight. They get their information from *you*—from you yourself—by adroit questioning, by playing on your emotions, by scaring and worrying you and then suddenly asking you a question. You blurt out the information they want. Then they hand your own information back to you as 'second sight.'"

Cherry nodded. It was true.

"But they *have* told me more things than I've foolishly revealed," Miss Kitty insisted.

Cherry suggested, "Maybe they dig up information about people in advance. You know, through newspapers or gossip or pumping your friends. That's easy to do. Then when you come in to see them, they can astound you by knowing all sorts of things about you."

"Certainly," Scott seconded her. "That's obviously the reason why your fancy and expensive Mr. Gregory Carroll insists that his 'clients' make appointments one and two weeks in advance. Gives him and the scholarly Mr. Thatch time to investigate you."

Miss Kitty sniffed. "We walked in on Miss Pride and that witch without advance appointments—without any warning at all—and they told us *exactly the same things* that Gregory Carroll told us!"

The three of them mused over this. Miss Owens argued that being told the identical things by three such various fortune–tellers "proved" the "truth" of fortune-telling.

"I don't believe it," the musician said stubbornly. "I can't think of a good explanation to refute you, Kit, but I don't believe it."

They went in to lunch in the diner, still arguing. The man with the magazine happened to be seated with them, since there were tables for two or for four. He did not join in their conversation, however. Later they saw him when they went to the observation car, and again back in their own Pullman. Once, when he jostled her as the train sped around a bend, Cherry was vaguely aware that she was growing tired of running into this man.

It was not until the final stop of the train ride, when the porter was carrying their bags out to the vestibule, and everyone was putting on hats and jackets, that Cherry took a good look at him. He was ordinary in appearance, with an underling's bearing, of medium height and build but very strong, thoroughly inconspicuous. The only distinguishing mark about him was that his left shoulder was a little higher than his right one.

CHAPTER VI

Reunion

THIS WEEK END WAS THE ONE CHERRY HAD BEEN WAITING for. The concert tour was successfully completed, and the musician had returned home to rest. Dr. Pratt, long before, had promised Cherry she might have this long week end off.

For this was a very particular date, ringed in red pencil on Cherry's calendar. A long-awaited date, long and earnestly prayed for, now excitedly prepared for by all the scattered Ameses, preceded by long-distance telephone calls between Cherry and her mother, and by a flurry of shopping for perfume and a comfortable new robe and slippers (and a winged piggy bank which Mr. Ames stuffed with quarters), crowned by the baking of an immense cake on which Mrs. Ames was right now squeezing out pink icing to spell: WELCOME HOME. For this was the week end Cherry's twin brother Charlie was to be mustered out of the Army Air Forces and—at last, at very long last—he would be home.

Hilton was drowsing under a July sun on the Saturday noon Cherry climbed her porch steps. She pushed her black curls off her warm forehead, feeling so excited she wondered if she were shooting off sparks. For not only was her adored brother arriving in state this week end—as if that were not happiness enough!—but Gwen and Mai Lee and the others were arriving today! This week end at the Ameses was to be the Spencer girls' big reunion—planned by letter, weeks ago, when Charlie was still a flying speck out in the Pacific. Charlie—her pals—holiday—

"It's like having a chocolate mint soda *and* a pecan fudge sundae *and* a whipped cream cake, all set before you at once," Cherry thought. "But I guess I can manage a double dose of pure happiness."

She dropped her small overnight bag with a thump in the hall and called:

"Hi, family! Here's another Ames! Where are you?"

Her mother called from the kitchen, "Come and admire Charlie's cake!"

Cherry raced through the cool, darkened rooms to the white kitchen. Mrs. Ames, flushed, was bending over the resplendent cake. Cherry kissed her hello.

"Welcome home to you, too," her mother said. "You look fine, honey. Dad and I were so pleased with your letters."

"I'm flourishing. Glad to see you are, too. Where's Dad? Oh, isn't this wonderful about Charlie?"

"Wonderful!"

Cherry and her pretty mother hugged each other in glee.

"Dad's downtown trying to buy Charlie some civilian clothes." Mrs. Ames untied her apron and smoothed her dress. "I have everything ready, finally, even myself!—Charlie's room, a nice lunch for your girls, rooms for them, tonight's picnic supper—"

"Poor Mother. Your kids certainly make you a lot of work."

"Oh, that's what mothers are for. I just hope—With such a houseful of youngsters already invited, if Charlie brings *his* friends too—Well, someone may end up sleeping in the bathtub!"

"Charlie's bringing a quartet of generals?" Cherry laughed.

"He wrote something about one young man he's very fond of—Oh! The ice cream! Cherry, run downtown this minute and get the gallon of peach Mr. Feldkamp is saving for me. And if you can find some green peppers," she called after Cherry, "and some more clothes hangers—And it wouldn't be a bad idea to buy extra toothbrushes—"

But Cherry was already halfway down the tree-lined block. She sped downtown in the scorching prairie heat, made the purchases for "Hotel Ames" plus

REUNION

Charlie's favorite red roses, plus gumdrops for Gwen, plus a pretty new compact for her long-suffering mother. Then Cherry raced home, juggling parcels, trying to trot along faster than the ice cream could melt. She arrived home in a litter of roses, toothbrushes, and curls in her eyes, and ducked straight into the shower. She scrubbed and showered and dressed herself into a presentable member of the family welcoming committee.

Not a minute too soon! The doorbell rang.

Cherry ran down the staircase, still clutching her hairbrush. Charlie? Gwen and the girls, bless 'em? Mrs. Ames got to the screen door first.

"We are selling a trial subscription to—" the man started.

"No, thank you," said Mrs. Ames forlornly.

"Then could I interest you in a free copy of our gardening bulletin which every household should—"

"Not today," said Mrs. Ames in a disappointed tone.

Cherry saw the salesman's expression turn sympathetic.

"If it's boll weevil in your garden that's making you feel bad, lady," he began—But Cherry good-naturedly waved her hairbrush at him and shooed him away.

"Now he'll probably tell our neighbors," Mrs. Ames said, "that we're a houseful of lunatics."

"Crazy with joy," Cherry agreed. She ran up the stairs and had reached the top landing when the doorbell shrilled again. Both Cherry and her mother made another wild dash toward the door.

It was Midge.

"Oh!" both Cherry and Mrs. Ames said. "Well, come in. Don't just *stand* there in this heat."

"You make me feel like an anticlimax," Midge protested. "You didn't notice my new hair-do, either. Listen, Cherry! What's the difference between a raven and a writing desk?"

"Don't know. Give up," Cherry said impatiently.

"You mean you don't know the difference betw—"

"This isn't exactly the right moment for puzzles, Midge dear," Mrs. Ames put in.

"Cherry doesn't even know *that*? Doesn't even know the difference between a raven and a writing desk?" Midge persisted. "My, I'll bet you have a lot of trouble when you sit down to write a letter." And Midge burst out laughing.

"I would describe you as a nuisance," Cherry said between clenched teeth, "if I weren't too polite to say such things."

Midge blinked, figuring that out. Mrs. Ames cocked her dark head. A car was stopping outside their house. It was a taxi, and Charlie and another khaki-clad airman were stepping out. Cherry rushed out on the porch, her brother ran up the porch steps four at a time. The Ames twins collided in a hug.

"Oh, Charlie! You old sweetie—"

"My favorite sister!"

"My favorite brother." She patted his fair hair. "The very nicest brother there is." Mrs. Ames crowded in, and Midge somehow squeezed in the middle.

"Home." Charlie looked at all of them, then lifted his eyes and looked at their gray house. "Home! Out of the Army Air Forces. For good." He grinned and stretched luxuriously. He was tall and athletic, light-haired, blue-eyed, and had exactly the same pert face as his sister. "Home ... Dad be home soon? ... I want to 'jest set' and look at all of you."

Mrs. Ames said, "Yes, I want you to rest, Charles."

Cherry was so delighted to see her brother that she sputtered. "You look pretty, I mean fine—was the Pacific a long way?—that is, did it take you long to get home?—Oh! you're still wearing the identification bracelet I gave you."

"Sure, honey. Never took it off for five years."

"Never? Not even once?"

"Not even once. Guess what, Cherry?" Charlie said. "I brought you an Oriental robe."

"That's wonderful. But you brought yourself, and that's the best present of all."

And they all said the commonplace, deeply felt phrases, and laughed a little for joy.

The other boy stood there, smiling and forgotten, until Charlie dragged him forward.

"—you are not either in the way. Mother—Cherry—*and* Midge—this is—All right, all right, I won't tell them. This is my good friend, Bucky Hall."

"How do you do, Bucky." Cherry still did not really notice him. She was too absorbed in the miracle of her brother's return from five years of combat flying. He and Bucky wore the same wings insignia on their khaki sleeves. They must have been through the same war experiences together. And here they were, having survived war together. No wonder they were close friends.

But Bucky remained, to Cherry, only Charlie's friend, only an anonymous flyer in khaki, until about half an hour later. Mr. Ames had come home, the preliminary tension was beginning to slacken, and they were all sitting around the living room, talking. Cherry overheard Midge say to Charlie's friend:

"What is it about you that Charlie isn't supposed to tell? Something awful?" she asked hopefully.

Bucky grinned. He had a crooked, likable grin. "My secret vice. I eat onions. Raw. For breakfast."

"That's no vice, that's a talent."

"Well, it certainly ensures my privacy. It worked even in the Army! The Fragrant Vagrant, they called me."

"On Kitchen Police, you were The Scallion Scullion," Charlie muttered. "Also, The Little Stinker."

"But confidentially, I eat onions for breakfast only in self-defense. Stop shuddering, Midge." Bucky's voice was husky, with an oddly plaintive note.

Cherry noticed now that Bucky Hall was one of the most attractive fellows she had ever seen. Not as tall as Charlie, not as handsome, nevertheless Bucky had a way about him. There was a cheerfulness about his turned-up nose, a swing to his walk, something teasing in his smile. He had so much charm that it was outrageous. But in disarming contrast, his eyes were soft and deep, and his voice had that plaintiveness.

Cherry said, liking him, "Onions or no onions, I trust you'll be here for breakfast tomorrow morning?"

"I'll be here for the weekend, thanks, but I can't guarantee that Hall will show up for breakfast. Unless Charlie blasts me awake. You wouldn't want me around *that* early, anyhow. I'm horrible, then. Cross, cranky, bite people's heads off—" Bucky grinned appealingly. "The rest of the time, of course, I'm lovely, just lovely. Practically a pin-up boy."

Charlie turned an affectionate, level gaze on his friend. "Bucky flew with me for a year. We got hurt together—that is, Bucky got hurt."

Cherry quickly turned to him.

Bucky scowled. "It was nothing. I—I just did it to get sympathy."

"He also got himself a couple of decorations," Charlie said meaningly.

"Will you go run up a tree?" Bucky demanded. "And why didn't you ever show me a really good picture of your sister? You know, Cherry, Charlie talked about you all the time. He bored us so much that we decided you were a battle-ax. I never suspected you'd be as nice as this."

"As nice as what?" Cherry teased.

"Cherry!" Midge said. She was shocked—and a bit jealous.

Bucky smiled at Cherry and his eyes were full of laughter. "I'll tell you over the weekend. In detail," he promised. "Very nice of all the Ameses to take me in. I'll try to be a model guest."

Cherry already thought Bucky Hall one of the most likable young men she had ever known. Having him around for the weekend, she decided, might be extremely pleasant.

For a moment Cherry nearly wished that the girls were coming some other weekend. But as she told Bucky about them—"warned" him, Charlie insisted—all their good times came dancing back. Swiping a life-sized doll—getting two of everything for a birthday-Christmas present, including a pair of galoshes—giving an Army party in the Pacific, and arranging Ann's wedding in England—all the funny, frolicking, heart-warming times together!

"Your girls sound grand," Bucky said. "But is this weekend going to be safe for mere males?"

Charlie urged flight before the oncoming feminine horde. He spoke, he said, from experience. Cherry knew her brother did not mean a word of his teasing. Bucky was all for holding his ground—even when, outside, a car door slammed and they could hear laughter.

"We'll vanish," Bucky gave in to Charlie, "but only while Cherry says hello to them. We'll be back later and with a vengeance! All right, Charlie? Come on, Midge, you're no more of a Spencer girl than I am."

Those three had already vanished out of Cherry's attention. A commotion started at the front door. "They're here!" Cherry shrieked and ran. "They're here!"

Young women spilled through the door. Redheaded Gwen Jones grabbed Cherry first. The others milled around them in the Ames living room.

"After all this time—you darlin' old so-and-so!"

"Hello, you old freckle face! You imp! Gosh, am I glad to see you. And Josie—Josie Franklin!"

Josie Franklin, looking like a frightened rabbit behind her glasses, wriggled forward. "We got back from England—I mean, we're here," she stuttered. "And—and—you see?"

"Yes, I see," Cherry laughed, kissing Josie, "and I'm darned glad you *are* here! Why, Bertha Larsen!"

A tall, plump, fair young woman enveloped Cherry in a large embrace. "This is nice," she said solemnly. "Only for such a good thing as this would I leave our farm."

"Next," said a Chinese-American girl shyly, from behind the others. Cherry swooped down on the demure ivory-faced figure, and Mai Lee suddenly turned into a real live person.

Cherry announced, "The others couldn't get here— Marie Swift is way out in San Francisco—Vivian is already job hunting, poor child—and Ann is very busy being Mrs. Jack Powell. It's a shame they couldn't come, because this is the first time we've met since we're out of uniform."

"Since we're out of the Army Nurse Corps."

"How long has it been?" someone asked.

"Whatever it is, it's too long!" Cherry said. "We've got to do something about keeping together. Starting right now!"

But first there were notes to exchange, notes of what each friend had been doing, and hoped to do. Cherry had last seen or heard of them all in England, in wartime. Ann and Gwen, with Cherry, had been flight nurses. The others had been attached to a mobile hospital unit. Like Cherry, several of them on their return to the United States had been veterans' nurses. Although their dress now was civilian, their talk rang of the martial nursing they had all so long and loyally worked at.

"I wish," said Mai Lee, "that I'd get a chance to wear a starched white uniform, for once in my life. Why, we've never—except for Cherry here—worn anything but student nurses' blue-and-white, and Army khaki!"

"Anyone heard from our old nursing superintendent, Miss Reamer?"

"She's fine, and she wrote me she wants us all to come back for a class reunion next year."

Josie Franklin was wailing, "But I don't *know* what I want to do next!"

"Me neither," said Gwen.

"So far, all of us are just resting after Army life," Bertha Larsen summed it up. "And trying to get our bearings."

"Well, there's one thing we're going to do!" Cherry said. She tossed back her curls. "We're not going to drift apart again. I've missed you kids like anything. So I propose—uh—I *declare* us the Spencer Club! As of this moment."

"Hear, hear!"

"Cherry for President!"

"No, no," Cherry said hastily. "We don't need a president or dues or regular meetings or anything. We'll just be a club for sticking-together purposes."

"An eating club would be nice," plump Bertha Larsen said hopefully.

"I could be corresponding secretary to stick us together," Josie Franklin offered.

"Unanimously accepted, Miss Franklin! We'll meet at least once a year, is that it, Cherry?"

Mai Lee said quietly, "Maybe we could all *do* something. Eight of us—counting in Ann and Marie and Vivian—all nurses—all making a fresh start in nursing—Maybe we could all go into the same field of nursing work together!"

"And all take an apartment together! Can you cook?"

"All right," Cherry said. "Next time that we *all* meet, a new career will be first on our agenda."

"Luncheon is on your agenda right now," said Mrs. Ames, coming in smiling. "My word, what eight girls will be able to think up! I thought our one nurse kept the household lively but a crowd of you—Well, this is fun!"

She led the chattering friends out into the side yard and garden. Bucky and Charlie were still tactfully keeping out of the way, Cherry noticed. Midge, too, was miraculously absent—probably as a result of maternal maneuvers.

On a picnic table under some shade trees, Mrs. Ames had spread a cool lunch. The girls took places on the two long benches, shooed a robin off the table, and feasted. The just-born Spencer Club relaxed and dismissed such matters as agendas and nursing careers. Their talk turned to romance.

"Where's Wade Cooper, Cherry? Aren't you going to marry him?"

"Ann Evans reports that marriage is grand!"

Gwen said in a stage whisper, "I strongly suspect Ann of being in love with her husband. But, Cherry, what about the handsome Captain Cooper?" Gwen groaned. "If only he'd fallen for me, freckles and all!"

"I like Wade, sure. But I have no overpowering urge to spend the rest of my life with him. I guess," Cherry said a little wistfully, "that I just haven't met the right man yet."

Bertha Larsen said, "Sometimes you find him in your own back yard, when you're not even looking for him. Right under your nose, Cherry."

Cherry jumped. Bertha was right! There was an eligible young man right under her nose. A young man named Bucky Hall.

"What about you, Bertha?" They all turned to the big fair girl.

Her china blue eyes softened. "About me—did I never tell you? It has been settled since I was a little girl, and John was a little boy on the farm next to ours. We grew up together, we always loved each other, we always knew we would marry. That is all."

There was a hush. Someone said, "That's very lovely."

"I am fortunate," Bertha said simply, but Cherry thought her John was the fortunate one. She herself began to feel rather forlorn. Apparently Josie Franklin did too, judging by her long face. Gwen was grinning to herself.

The girls pounced on Gwen. "What about you?"

Gwen flushed. "He lives in St. Louis. Nothing serious, honestly. We're just in the 'I-could-dance-with-you-forever' stage."

"Well," said Bertha practically, "when you get to the 'could-you-care-for-me-forever' stage, be sure to let us all know. We'll give you a shower."

Cherry said, "St. Louis? I'm going there soon with my Owenses. We'll be at the Mississippi Hotel."

"Oh, fine! I'm going to be in St. Louis visiting my aunt and"—Gwen grinned—"guess-who. It's a date, Cherry."

Josie Franklin blurted out, "Nobody loves me, only my mother. It's my glasses, I know it is!"

"Take off your glasses," someone suggested.

"And part your hair on the side," Cherry suggested. "There, that's more becoming."

"But I can't see!" Josie whimpered. "Or isn't that important?"

"Wear cute glasses. I saw a girl in a red sports coat and glasses with red frames, and a little red hair bow, and she looked darling."

"And your clothes are always too baggy, Josie. Stand up. See, it should fit neatly at the shoulders and at the waistline, *here*." Josie looked surprised to find that she owned a waistline.

The Spencer Club, working with pins, a borrowed belt, a donated scarf, a comb, deft fingers, and a sense of line and color, calmly proceeded to make over Josie Franklin on the side lawn.

They had just finished remodeling Josie when Cherry became aware of two interested spectators squatting beside the grape arbor. The two fellows were rocking with silent laughter, and pretending to primp their hair and powder their noses.

"Have you two fellows been there all along?" Cherry called over.

"Oh dear, yes indeedy," her brother called back in falsetto, and Bucky daintily leaned over Charlie and draped his khaki tie around his ear.

"Don't we look sweet?" Bucky inquired. "We're the glamour goons!"

"You wretches!" Cherry was exasperated but she could not help laughing. "Come over here and be introduced."

"Oh, we couldn't possibly, rai-eelly, we're too, too naked without our chartreuse nail polish!"

"And my di-*vine* mustache hasn't come back from the dry cleaner's!"

"The meanies!" Josie Franklin said, and looked as if she might rain tears. "The absolute meanies!"

By this time all the girls were laughing. The young men strolled over grinning, Bucky fixing a grape leaf rakishly in his hair. When they arrived at the picnic table where the five girls sat, their manner changed.

Bucky bowed from the waist. "*Chères demoiselles*, I am zo 'appy. Thees ees—'ow you say?—the snappiest moment of my wife—I mean life. Or something."

Charlie, who already knew his sister's pals, said gravely, "May I present the French ace, Henri Henri. His middle name is also Henri but he doesn't want to overdo it. M'sieu Henri, tell us—"

The girls smothered giggles. Mai Lee said pleasantly: "*Dîtes-moi, M'sieu Henri, venez-vous de Paris, France, ou de Paris, Illinois?*"

"Huh?" said the alleged French ace. "How's that again?"

Midge slipped out from behind the big oak tree, and sniffed. "*Et pourquoi avez-vous* left me in the lurch? Ne *m'aimez-vous pas?*" she demanded. "*Ou suis-je plus jeune?*—AS USUAL!"

Charlie whispered hoarsely, "Tell 'em your French poem, Buck—Henri."

Bucky smiled ingratiatingly at one and all. "*Mais oui. Oui, certainement. Oui, oui.*" He cleared his throat and recited:

> "*Je vous aime,*
>   *Je vous adore,*
> *Que voulez-vous*
>   *L'encore?*"

There was applause.

Midge sniffed a second time. "Your French accent sounds like peanuts going through the roaster."

"You simply don't appreciate me," Bucky said. "But all fooling aside, will somebody name names or do I have to call you, 'Hey, you!'"

"You might hit us over the head with a crowbar, if you want to attract our attention," Gwen suggested. She nudged Cherry, "Run right out and get M'sieu Henri a nice, fresh crowbar. Oh, *very well!* I'm Gwen Jones, spelled Jones."

"And Josie," Cherry said, "Mai Lee, and Bertha."

Bucky grinned at all of them and said:

"Now Charlie Ames will entertain with *his* recitation."

Charlie's blue eyes looked blank for a moment. Then he struck a pose and declaimed:

> *"The organ pealed potatoes,*
> *'Lard' was rendered by the choir,*
> *The sexton, rung the dishrag,*
> *Someone set the church on fire.*
>
> *'Holy smoke!' the preacher shouted,*
> *In the fire he lost his hair;*
> *Now his head resembles heaven,*
> *For there is no parting there."*

This was well received. Then they teamed up for The Game—silently acting out phrases. Bucky's team led off with "Minors not allowed." Midge was histrionic as a miner, "not" was knotting everything they could lay hands on, and for "allowed" they pantomimed beating drums, shouting, and covering their ears with their hands for "loud." Cherry's team responded with "Sunny Side Up." Charlie was "Sonny," toddling around with knees bent after his "mother," Mai Lee. For "side," Cherry, Charlie, Mai Lee, and Josie all lay down in the grass, side by side, on their sides. They wobbled with laughter while the other team guessed "corpses, sausages, four, down" and "they've gone crazy!" and finally caught on when Cherry repeatedly pointed to her side. Bucky's team stymied Cherry's team with "Duncan Phyfe"—acting out "dunk," "in," and for "fife," strenuously miming the famous Revolutionary trio, waving flag, drummer, bandage over the eye, fife, and all. Cherry's team was violently enacting David and Goliath, and tossing pennies about and impersonating policemen—to build up to "David Copperfield"—when Mrs. Ames called them.

"Are you hungry enough yet for the picnic supper?"

"Oh, sure, always hungry!" Bucky sang out, then looked embarrassed. "Mrs. Ames, can we help you?"

"No, thanks, everything is ready."

"Good," Bucky said candidly. "I hate helping. But I will, I will, Mrs. Ames. It's my better nature creeping up on me, darn it."

How Mr. and Mrs. Ames, Cherry, Gwen, Josie, Bertha, Mai Lee, Charlie, Bucky, and Midge all piled into the family sedan (named Nellie) was inexplicable. It took them some time and experimenting to achieve. Neighbors gathered at their porch rails to watch and to call packing suggestions. Midge fell out once. Finally the parents and the two boys squeezed into the front seat, and the six girls filled the back to the roof. When they were all in, Mrs. Ames remembered she had left the two immense hampers of food sitting on the step, and where would they put them anyway?

Mr. Ames shut off the engine and said wearily:

"Look here. I will whistle bird calls, Charlie can strew papers and peanut shells over the lawn, and the rest of you can jostle one another. That way, we can stay right in our own front yard and still have all the discomforts of the picnic grounds."

There was polite, pained silence. No one moved. Mrs. Ames suggested inviting Mr. Ames out of the car and putting in the hampers instead. Everyone got hungrier and hungrier. The sun set, the discussion continued.

"Excuse me," Midge said, and wormed her way out of the car.

She went over to the hampers, opened one, extracted a sandwich, and—before the assembled company—munched.

"I can't wait," Midge said, unabashed.

"Neither can I," admitted Bucky. "Yippee! I'm starved."

"Will somebody kindly hit me with a hard-boiled egg?" Gwen said.

Mr. Ames declared this an emergency, and they picnicked in the yard. Three small boys showed up, over the back fence, to help them dispose of the ice cream. A dog and two cats also joined their party. They ate and laughed and joked, until a huge round yellow moon hung in the tree branches like a lantern.

Bucky, Cherry found, had somewhere in the proceedings established himself at her side.

"I have things to say to you," he said. "Such as, you look like a battle-ax in your brother's snapshots, but you turn out to be my idea of a gorgeous—"

"Never mind," Cherry interrupted, laughing.

He whispered in her ear, "I have to be attentive to my hostess, don't I? M'sieu Henri is always polite."

Cherry supposed that was the plain truth, but her heart preferred not to believe it.

The other girls demanded to know what Cherry and Bucky were whispering about.

Bucky's answer was, "Let's all go swimming."

"Swimming at night?"

"That's the best time."

Down to the river trooped the six nurses and the two young men. After renting bathhouses and changing into bathing suits, they ran along the sand, cold now without the sun, and splashed into the broad, deep Wabash River. The water felt cool, almost cold, and silky. Night sky and night water were so dark that they were all merely pale blurs, voices.

Charlie and Bucky saw to it that each of the six ladies was thoroughly ducked. Then they started a long, steady swim out to the anchored float. They were not much inclined to talk, with the prairie moon lighting the wake they kicked up, and outlining their half-seen faces. A quiet mood settled over them. There was Bucky, swimming along, again at Cherry's side.

At the float, they climbed out of the water, and sat dripping and shivering a little on the rocking raft. They sang, they talked a bit. But mostly they watched and felt the magic of the summer night.

And Bucky said to Cherry, lightly but very low, "I certainly have things to say to you, Princess."

CHAPTER VII

Romance in Reverse

BRIGHT AND EARLY SUNDAY MORNING, THERE WAS A loud banging on the girls' doors.

"Get up!" Charlie called. "The sun is shining and we're going to the county fair!"

The only protest at being awakened early came from Bucky, as he staggered down the stairs. Even Midge, who had stayed overnight at the Ameses, willingly yawned herself awake. None of the girls had slept much the night before. Who wanted to sleep, as Gwen said, when they could visit—they could sleep some other time. Part of their talk had consisted of wails at Cherry: "Lucky—to have Bucky falling for you!"

"Oh, no," Cherry had said modestly. "He's just being nice to me because I'm his hostess."

But she convinced no one, not even herself. The girls' teasing planted the idea in Cherry's head. She fell asleep thinking of Bucky's crooked grin.

And now, in the test of broad daylight, with Bucky gallantly putting cream and sugar in her coffee for her, Cherry looked at him with increased interest. He certainly was a darling. Maybe he did like her. Maybe her friends were right. Well, she would wait and see what today would bring. And if it brought her a real conquest of Bucky, that would be very, very nice!

"Don't get all mushy and woozy, Ames," she warned herself. "Remember, you've been working so long and hard that practically any nice young man would look awfully good to you."

But Bucky really was someone special, and it was hard to hold on to her heart when he whispered to her:

"Do you always look so ravishing first thing in the morning? Good grief, most gals I've seen at this hour look like tired dishrags. You have roses in your cheeks and your eyes are shiny and—gee, you're even civil at breakfast!"

"Ever been to a county fair?"

"Don't change the subject. Why won't you take me seriously?"

"They have pigs and carrousels and side shows."

"All right, Cherry, I'll take you for a ride on everything. On one condition."

"Oh, I'm in fine condition, thanks," Cherry giggled.

"Look, Princess, we're speaking English. I think— Listen, Cherry, the condition is this: Will you let me ask you a question? Later on? I really am stuck for an answer."

Cherry was amazed but kept it to herself. "That will cost you one ferris wheel ride extra."

"Sold."

Charlie drove up in the family car. Giggling and in high spirits, the girls tumbled into it. They set off along green country roads for an all-day jaunt to the fair.

In a big stretch of trees they found cars parked hundreds deep, saw a maze of wire-fenced streets and wooden buildings, heard the barkers and the tinny music of the merry-go-round. A ferris wheel rose in outline against the brilliant blue sky.

"Me for the flower show!" Mai Lee exclaimed as they tumbled out of their parked car.

"I want to see the prize livestock," Bertha Larsen said. "And the preserving and baking exhibits."

"And the handmade bedspreads and quilting," Josie squealed.

Both men groaned. What they wanted was to see the rodeo.

"But that isn't until this afternoon," Cherry said, consulting a handbill. "Let's just start walking and do everything as we come to it, mm?"

They strolled along in the festive fairgrounds. Crowds had already gathered. Messrs. Ames and Hall gallantly endowed their six ladies with spun candy on sticks and a carrousel ride, to open proceedings. They paused to admire the cows, became acquainted with the horses, and met a prize pig.

"Pig looks like you, Hall," Charlie declared.

"He does not!" Cherry defended him indignantly.

"You mean the pig is better looking?" Midge said bitterly. She could not forgive Bucky for paying all his compliments to Cherry and none to her.

Bucky laughed and said he knew a way to settle it—if Josie would use her camera. They took a snapshot of Bucky and the pig together. "Both smiling," Josie said.

"Let's all have our pictures taken," Bertha proposed. "While our faces are still clean."

They wandered over to the carnival grounds of the fair, stopping for pink lemonades on the way. The photographer's barker spotted them coming.

"Step right this way—ladeez and gen'mum—have your pitcha taken! A bee-yoo-tee-ful group pitcha for on'y fifty cents, on'y half of a single li'l dollah!"

The eight of them entered the booth and debated whether to be immortalized, on cardboard, waving merrily from a paper motorboat or smiling sugarily from a moth-eaten cottage door. Bucky wanted to stand before a hula girl figure made of paper, with his head atop and holding Cherry's hand. The pictures came out as horrors, as they expected. Everyone kept a copy, anyhow.

ROMANCE IN REVERSE 121

Side shows kept them busy for the next hour. Midge was so horribly fascinated by the snake charmer that she could swallow no lunch. But the rest of them cheerfully ruined their digestions with hot dogs and corn on the cob and ice cream. Games of skill were next. Bucky shot arrows and won a kewpie doll and a collar box. He tenderly presented both to Cherry. She tried to look thrilled with these objects, but her pleasure at Bucky's attentiveness was real enough. In the confusion of the crowd, Gwen muttered to her:

"Bucky certainly is all yours—you lucky thing!"

Cherry smiled, and shook her head. "M-m, he *is* a charmer, isn't he?"

Mai Lee said, "You know you love every minute of it. And who wouldn't!"

Midge and Josie mourned together that Cherry had all the luck. "Of course, Cherry, you are nice—we mean—" The only one who made no comment was her brother—to Cherry's relief. She did not mean to provoke his unmerciful teasing if she could help it.

Rodeo—more side shows—more sticky, sweet, awful things to eat and drink—and for grand climax, the ferris wheel.

They paired off for the ferris wheel. Bucky and Cherry first, hand in hand. Then Charlie and Mai Lee, whom Charlie particularly admired. Gwen and Bertha climbed into the next swinging two-seater, and Midge and Josie comprised a disgruntled rear guard.

The wheel started to turn, and Cherry and Bucky gently soared up into the air. From here, the whole, vivid, milling fairgrounds spread beneath their gaze. Up and up the wheel carried them, into the dazzling sky. Sounds below dimmed, and they had a delicious sense of privacy. It was an almost secret pleasure. They smiled at each other, and when the wheel carried them to the ground, and the others got out, Bucky refused to budge.

"We're going around and around again, Cherry. Indefinitely," he announced.

The others cried, "Hurry up! Or we'll go off and leave you!"

"Fine," Bucky said. After that answer, no one moved.

Charlie and company had a long wait, a very long wait. The ferris wheel got stuck. Bucky and Cherry were stranded at the very top.

"This is awful!" Cherry leaned over the edge of their car and looked down on her friends' distant, disgusted faces.

"This is very nice," Bucky corrected her. "Shall we talk? Shall I sing for you? Wish I had a long string and a hook. We could fish people's hats off. Then we could go into the millinery business. Then we would grow very, very rich, and live happily ever after."

"Stuck in the sky with a madman!"

Bucky said plaintively, "The only trouble is, we didn't bring blankets. It's going to get cold up here around midnight. Moral: Always carry blankets."

"Do you honestly think we're going to be stuck here all night?" Cherry was not as alarmed as she sounded.

Bucky pulled a melting piece of chewing gum out of his pocket and gave it to her with a flourish. "This is for the kewpie doll, not you. Relax, Princess. I'll tell you the story of my life, and what beautiful black eyes you have, Grandmother."

This nonsense went on, to the accompaniment of hammering below on the ferris-wheel machinery, and intermittent shouts and facemaking by Charlie, for the rest of the afternoon. Bucky said a number of highly tantalizing things.

"Just wait till I catch you this evening in the moonlight, in the starlight, in the lovelight, in the porch swing," he whispered in the car, as they drove home. "Have to be attentive to my hostess, you know!"

"You're an outrageous flirt!" she hissed back.

"No, it's just high spirits. But you like it, don't you?"

Yes, she did like Bucky, Cherry admitted to herself. She regretted that they were all so dog-tired that evening, and her friends so omnipresent. Her tête-à-tête with Bucky in the porch swing might prove exciting if it materialized. Cherry wished it would.

Bucky took the situation in hand. He shooed everyone away, announcing that he and Cherry were "in conference."

It was anything but a business conference. The moon shone down on them and flowers bloomed at their shoulder. Bucky paid Cherry some extravagant compliments, which sounded thrilling in the moonlight. Suddenly he grew thoughtful. "About that question, Cherry."

"Yes, Bucky," Cherry gently encouraged.

"Well, it's this," he smiled warmly. "What do you think would be a nice present for a very nice girl?"

She held her breath. "I suppose that would depend on what the girl is like, wouldn't it?"

"She's lovely," Bucky said softly.

Cherry smiled at him. "No doubt she likes you, too," she encouraged.

"I certainly hope so! Now, let's see—"

"You don't want to spend too much," said Cherry, careful of a young man's pocket. "I'm sure I—she—wouldn't want too grand a gift."

"I'd spend my last dollar for her," Bucky said earnestly. "Do you think she'd like a wrist watch? Or a ring—the most beautiful ring I could find?"

Cherry was thrilled. She stammered, "Do you know what size she wears?" She was playing for time, trying to think. This had come so suddenly.

"No, I don't know her size."

"Couldn't you find out?"

"Well, she's smaller than you—"

Cherry stiffened in surprise. "Smaller," she echoed weakly.

"I said, she's smaller than you. Quite tiny. And golden-haired," Bucky went on in the same soft, confiding voice. "Seems silly not to know my fiancée's size, but I haven't seen her for a year, I've forgotten her sizes."

"Oh," said Cherry. It was all she could think of to say. *His fiancée. Golden-haired. Smaller than you.*

"You'd love her, Cherry. Peg and I—her name's Peg—we always like the same people. You'd love her."

"I'm sure I would." Cherry forced a weak smile.

"Well, now, isn't that nice of you! Come on. Help me decide on what to give her," Bucky rattled on cheerfully and unconsciously. "She's golden haired and tiny, as I said, if that's any help to you."

No help whatsoever, Cherry thought glumly. But she made herself say that golden jewelry should be very nice with golden hair. And she bade the grateful Bucky a rather hasty good night.

Upstairs, the girls' jokes about Cherry's "conquest" of Bucky did not make her feel any better. When they asked her, "What did he say?" and "Did you let him kiss you?"—disillusion settled over her like a cold rain in the middle of vacation.

"Ho, hum!" Cherry stifled her feelings with a large pretended yawn. "It's a bright, moonlight night, but right now I could use some sleep," she evaded.

Monday morning Cherry felt miserable as she drove the Spencer Club down to the railroad station. Even as they boarded the train, the Club was still heatedly discussing its future.

"We'll meet soon again and decide then."

"Now that we've started our Spencer Club, we're going to go through with it!"

"See you in St. Louis, Cherry!"

"See you, Gwen."

Cherry drove back home alone. The family was nowhere in sight. Her mother had left a note, saying Bucky was gone, bag and baggage, and said good-bye and thanks to her. Cherry was relieved that she did not have to see him again.

She wandered around the deserted rooms, sourly thinking, "What a fool I made of myself! Lucky, huh? Conquest, huh? Why, he told me in so many words that he was merely being polite! Just doing his duty to his hostess! And I—I—I threw myself at him!"

Covered with chagrin, Cherry felt like the well-known two cents. If that much. How Bucky must have laughed at her, as she dangled like a popeyed fish on the bait of his compliments. Well, why had he called her Princess—tagged after her everywhere—made her believe he was smitten? It wasn't fair!

But, on second thought, Cherry had to admit that Bucky had not led her on. She had taken too much for granted. It was her friends who had led—or misled—her on. Not Bucky! Even stuck up there in the ferris wheel, his golden opportunity to get sentimental,

Bucky had merely been his entertaining self. She decided grimly that at least he had to be credited with delightful manners. He had simply repaid hospitality by being as amiable as he knew how.

"Nevertheless, I hate him! Making a monkey of me!"

A small silent voice squeaked: "You made a monkey of yourself. And you certainly did a thorough job of it!"

Cherry threw herself on the couch, dug her heels in the upholstery, and moped. "Sunk," she muttered. "Completely sunk. You gosh-darn fool!"

Suddenly the spectacle of herself fluttering coyly after a young man who was—romantically—blissfully unconscious of her, struck her funny. She started to laugh, silently at first, then roared out loud.

But the sore spot was still there, and she still was annoyed with herself. She realized her lightheaded foolishness was a natural reaction after being tied down so long on the Owens case. But she hoped to goodness her brother had not noticed, and that the friends would not learn the truth, or she would never hear the end of this!

"What a sucker I am! What a gullible—"

Mrs. Ames came in, her arms full of groceries.

"What are you looking so depressed about, Cherry?"

"Ohh—nothing."

"Your friends are sweet. And that Bucky is very charming.

"Entirely too charming."

"Why, Cherry!" Her mother studied her with shrewd and understanding eyes. "Hmm. That reminds me. Did you find the letter for you from Wade Cooper?"

Cherry brightened a little. "From Wade?"

"It came last Thursday and I put it on the hall table with the rest of the mail. Didn't you find it?"

"No, I didn't. And I want it! Quick!"

Mrs. Ames sighed. "I suspect Midge would know where it is. Midge and her grand passion for Captain Cooper."

Cherry telephoned Midge.

"Why, yes, I do have Wade's letter at that," Midge admitted airily. "I was kind of sort of keeping it for you. I saw Wade's name on the envelope and—it's been such a satisfaction to have it in my pocket!"

Wade's letter, when rescued and opened, read:

"Dear Cherry—So you thought you were through with me, and vice versa, did you? Well, so did I. And boy, are we both wrong!"

"I forgive you for everything, even rescuing me from drowning."

"Papa Cooper herewith notifies you that only a love affair with your rival, the auto repair business, keeps him away from you. But I will be around eventually, and that's for sure. Don't you dare even look at anyone else."

"Your ever-loving, long-suffering,
Wade."

Cherry forgot about Bucky fast and thoroughly.

CHAPTER VIII

The Threat

THE INSTANT CHERRY STEPPED INSIDE THE OWENS house, she sensed that something was wrong.

Jen, who had let her in, wore an anxious air. Octave the cat paced the piano top, a nervous barometer of the house's mood. Worst of all, there was no music—only strained silence.

"Miss Cherry, I certainly am relieved you're here!" the housekeeper exclaimed. "I'll take your bag. You run right upstairs to Mr. Scott."

"What's wrong?" Cherry asked fearfully. "Is he sick? Was Dr. Pratt called?"

Jen shook her white head. "Not sick, but I'm afraid he may be. Something awful has happened, he's had a shock, he and Miss Kitty look like ghosts. No, I haven't the faintest notion of what it is. Go along now, run."

Cherry ran.

On the second floor, the doors to the two Owenses' bedrooms and to Miss Kitty's office stood open. The rooms were deserted. Cherry fled past the third floor where her own bedroom and the guest chamber were located. On the fourth floor, where she had never been before, she still heard no voices to guide her.

Cherry hesitated, then knocked on the door of the room which faced the street. No answer. Gingerly she turned the knob and looked in. She discovered Scott Owens's workroom—a grand piano heaped with music scores, some printed, some in pencil, and a piano bench and a powerful lamp, nothing more.

Cherry turned across the hall and paused before the other closed door. Yes, here she heard sibilant whispers. She knocked.

Miss Kitty opened the door a crack. "Miss Cherry! Back so soon?" Her face looked pinched and old. "Well, isn't that nice. Why don't you go to your room and rest, or have some tea, or—ah—"

"Let her come in," Scott Owens called weakly. "She might as well know."

"I don't want to intrude—" But Miss Kitty flung the door open, drew Cherry in, and closed the door once more, as if she were closing out trouble. Cherry found herself in the musician's study. If the musician himself had been in a better mood, this would have been an inspiring and fascinating room, she reflected. All

THE THREAT

four walls were covered with framed photographs of the great in music, of all continents, and some in other arts, all inscribed affectionately to Scott. The names were dazzling. A fine gray marble fireplace, banked with green leaves for the summer months, had on its mantel gifts and curios collected on Scott's musical travels. A great basket of red roses, tagged with an admirer's card, nodded between the two ceiling-high windows. But the blinds were closed, and Scott Owens lay back on one of the divans in exhaustion.

He sat up a little as Cherry approached and tried to smile at her.

"Hello, my little nurse, did you have a good time?"

"Yes, thanks, but *you*, Mr. Scott—"

"No, I'm not ill, just terribly worried. I've had a bad upset. Bad."

Miss Kitty nervously fingered her reddish hair. "Do you really think, Scott, that you ought to tell about—"

"*You* told! *You* talked too much, didn't you? To the wrong people—with this wretched result!" His thin, usually gentle face was fiery. His sister sat down and bit her lips. "You sit down too, Cherry, and listen. Unless you don't care about listening to this mess?"

"I do care, Mr. Scott! Not about your secrets," Cherry stammered, "about your health."

She was indeed concerned about the effects of shock and worry on her cardiac patient.

The musician's bottomless eyes stared ahead for a long minute. His voice shook a little as he started to talk.

"You remember the various fortunetellers we went to? You particularly remember Gregory Carroll in the fancy apartment? Carroll," he sneered, "with his 'saintly' air, and his much too clever secretary, Mr. Thatch, and—yes, and that harpsichord which they probably *rented* to win my sympathies!"

Miss Kitty mumbled, "Don't excite yourself, Scott. Please."

"Don't excite myself!" he shouted. "My Lord, we're on the verge of ruin—*of public disgrace*—and she tells me—"

"What's happened?" Cherry broke in quickly.

"Blackmail! And may the Lord help us!"

Cherry repeated disbelievingly, "Blackmail—Gregory Carroll is threatening you—threatening to—"

Scott Owens covered his eyes with his hands. "It's the end of my career—of my good name—of our income—of our whole life—" He waved his hand at the walls with their photographs. "It's the end of everything!"

Miss Kitty was noisily crying into a tiny handkerchief.

Cherry took a deep breath. Someone had to remain calm, to steady these two panic-stricken people. It was up to her. Yet she felt herself to be on very delicate ground. To reason them out of their terrible mood, she would have to discuss their most private affairs, ask questions, pry—and she had no right to do that.

THE THREAT

The whole idea of meddling was distasteful to Cherry. Yet here they sat, helpless, alone, gone to pieces emotionally. She ventured to ask exactly what Carroll had threatened.

Miss Owens drew up her big frame in the chair. She said heavily, "I'll tell you what he wants. That fortuneteller found out something in my brother's past which, if made public, could ruin him. We've guarded that secret for years—how he found it out, I still don't know—"

"You told him, you fool," Scott said bitterly.

"Yes, Scott, I admit I did tell him bits of it. And I suppose, as you said on the train that day, these fortunetellers know how to dig up confidential information."

Cherry suddenly, sharply remembered their talk on the train, and the man who had sat opposite them. Had he listened? Had they said anything compromising? What idiots they had been to discuss anything private, in public!

"—has dug up all these facts, you see," Miss Kitty was continuing, "and now Carroll threatens to—"

"Just a minute," Cherry interrupted. "Has he *proof*?"

There was an odd silence. Scott answered:

"We don't know."

"But we certainly think so. Otherwise how would he dare threaten us?"

"Bluffing you?" Cherry suggested.

But Scott sadly shook his head. "I'm afraid not. And this is what he wants. Listen to this! Carrol demands that in return for keeping his mouth shut, I pay him ten thousand dollars! My Lord, I haven't *got* it!"

"And if you start paying him, you'll pay for the rest of your life," his sister said. She started to cry again. "Don't think that extortion stops with one payment!"

Cherry rubbed her cheek with her fist, trying to think. She felt sickened at what the Owenses had just told her. They were caught tight in the clutches of an unscrupulous man—a racketeer who would coldly take away Scott's music, house, health, even his honorable name, unless Scott gave him money, for years and years to come. No wonder the two veins at the sides of Scott's thin neck throbbed so hard that Cherry could see them beating.

"I know what I'd do in such a predicament," Cherry thought aloud. "I'd report this threat to the police at once."

An unexpected reaction met her words. Miss Kitty laughed. And Scott said, "Cherry, you're naive."

With a jolt, Cherry understood. They *could not* go to the police for protection, because some fact in Scott's past really was disgraceful. They would rather face Gregory Carroll and his threats than own up to that fact. They needed to keep it hidden at any cost. Whatever it was, it must be extremely serious.

THE THREAT

So Scott really had been in bad trouble! Scott, who was so gentle and impractical. Cherry found it hard to believe and still could not believe Scott himself was bad.

What had he done? Cherry racked her brains, her memory. That uncle who must never be mentioned before the artist—money—proof in a box—a different name, possibly—Cherry fleetingly thought of all sorts of crimes, of punishment, disgrace, suffering—

Scott was suffering now. He was ill with suffering. One glance at his gray face told that; another indication was such irritability, coming from a normally sweet-tempered person. Cherry thought he could easily be on the verge of a heart attack. One more prod from Carroll, one more worry added to the load already burdening him, and his overwrought nerves and frail body would crack.

"Mr. Scott, you'd better go to bed, or at least lie down," Cherry said. "I'm going to call up Dr. Pratt and ask him to have a look at you."

But her patient begged to talk a little longer, saying that he could not rest with this terror on his mind. Cherry saw this was true enough, and relented.

"Maybe I should go to the police," he wavered. "You see, Cherry, I didn't—Believe me, I've done foolish things, mistaken things, ignorant ones—but on my word of honor, I've never intentionally done anything evil." He seemed hopeful for a moment, then fell back on the divan again. "But if the facts were made public, the world would believe only the worst of me. No, it's hopeless. And what would become of Kit, if all this were spread all over the newspapers—in the gossip columns—everything raked up from years ago—I can just see the blackest, most lurid headlines—" He groaned and fell silent.

Miss Kitty ventured, "If you could be cleared—"

"Yes, there are those papers. In the box. In the vault box."

Cherry's heart leaped with hope. "Proof to clear you! The box the 'witch' was trying to locate? On Carroll's instructions, do you suppose?"

"Possibly, who knows," the pianist said wearily. "There *is* proof of a sort, in our safety deposit box in a bank vault, right here in this city." But he did not say which bank. He went on to talk vaguely about the proof, and Cherry's hopes evaporated as he explained. It was a guarded explanation, revealing nothing of Scott's secret past. Scott merely stated that proof did not weigh very heavily against unfavorable publicity. "Plant an ugly idea in people's minds," he said, "and they won't bother to verify whether it's true or not."

"But won't those papers help even a little?" Miss Kitty said in a confused way. "I mean, then Carroll at least couldn't say—"

"No, no, no! Carroll can't be stopped by a few old documents."

THE THREAT

"Maybe if *I* went to speak to Gregory Carroll—" Miss Kitty said. "After all, I pride myself on being a practical person—" Scott stopped her with a harsh laugh. "Or no, if we could get hold of Mr. Thatch and win his confidence—" She went on making bootless suggestions. She merely tangled up the issue further. And the more she talked, the more upset her brother became.

Cherry decided it was time for someone to take a firm hold of the situation.

"See here," she said. "This aimless talking will get us nowhere. You'll have to come to a decision, the sooner the better. No matter what in the past is worrying you, I still suggest you at least *consult* the police about this, even if you don't want them to take action. After all, a crime is being perpetrated against you. The very least you can do is report it. Decide yes or no, about going to the police. That's the first step."

Miss Kitty discreetly held her tongue. Scott could not decide. He worried over Cherry's suggestion, hesitated, wavered, worried some more. He was too upset to think clearly.

Cherry saw this and determinedly rose to her feet. She went over to the musician. "Now this is enough fretting! You will make a yes-or-no decision by tomorrow morning, agreed? Come along now, Mr. Scott. I'm your nurse and in charge of you. You're going to your room and rest."

The musician followed her gratefully, out to the little one-passenger elevator in the stair well, and descended. Cherry went back to speak to Miss Kitty, but the sister already had gone downstairs.

Well, something had been accomplished, Cherry felt. She had cut short Miss Kitty's useless, upsetting talk—had cut short Mr. Scott's worrying—had defined the situation by asking for a decision. Scott would decide by morning. They could act constructively from that point. Relieved, Cherry went on downstairs.

Bébé was alone in the living room. Although Cherry was in no mood for a visitor, she could not help grinning at this fat, jolly man.

"Miss Cherry," he said and laboriously bowed. "To see you again, it is nice."

"Nice to see you, Mr. Bébé. Yes, I have a minute. Several minutes. Sit down and talk to me," she said politely.

"I am so sorry I say you smell by accident. You are angry, no?"

"No."

"I repologize. Say it, I cannot very good. My words mix up like spaghetti. I play it how sorry I am."

He waddled gallantly to the first piano. Cherry tried not to smile.

"I play for you somesing a young man writes on a summer evening, because he was with love all filled up. You, also, are young and you, also—I *hope*—to have much fine love. So! I play! Mendelssohn's *Midsummer Night's Dream* music, for the play by Shakespeare."

He sat down and played. Spun dreams tumbled out in the airiest, laciest music. From Bébé's pudgy fingers, elves and fairies emerged and scampered, leaves rustled and blew their fragrance, moons shimmered, young lovers sought each other in an enchanted night forest, and the little woodland animals danced for joy.

Cherry listened, transported, to the melody which soared lightly on, and rippled off to nothing under Bébé's fingers.

"You like?"

Cherry let out a big sigh. "Ah-h! Play it again."

"No, but— Mm—ah—boogie woogie, you like?"

"Do I? I'm mad about it! But do you play jazz?"

Bébé's round face glowed. "In strict confidentially, Scott showed me to play it. Now! I play! Hokay! *Movin' The Boogie*."

He attacked the keyboard with the full force of his shoulders. Now the piano became, not a simulated orchestra as in the Mendelssohn overture, but an instrument in its own right: a percussion instrument. And the way Bébé played now, the piano sounded like an entirely new and different musical instrument. Bébé's left hand beat out a powerful, rhythmic, drumlike bass, while from his right hand wound the complex threads of a plaintive melody. It was loud, strong, overpowering, all motion.

140 *CHERRY AMES, PRIVATE DUTY NURSE*

Bébé perspired and beamed. In perfect American he shouted at Cherry, "This boogie sure is movin'!"

Cherry's feet, head, whole body kept time to the dogged rhythms. They were both thoroughly enjoying themselves. The music beat on, pounding and rushing ahead like a locomotive on a railroad track—until Miss Owens came to the door and shouted, "Cherry! Scott's had a heart attack!"

The music stopped instantly.

"Mr. Thatch was just here, relaying Carroll's threat again—and that did it! Scott keeled over in my office—hurry!"

Cherry and Miss Kitty raced upstairs.

In the office, the musician was lying on the floor. He was conscious and trying to clutch his left side with his right hand. His left arm lay twisted in pain. He saw Cherry and struggled to raise his head.

"No, no, lie down." Cherry knelt beside him. "Keep perfectly still."

His face was ashen and he was covered with clammy sweat. He tried to speak but could not. Cherry knew he was in agonizing pain—pain which pressed against his heart, wrenched through his left shoulder and crippled the whole left arm temporarily. Scott was in mental agony, too, Cherry knew, suffering a sense of impending death.

"Here, breathe this." Hastily she dug into her pocket for the sealed glass tube of amyl nitrite, which she had carried on her person day and night ever since she became Scott Owens's nurse. She broke the perle inside her clean handkerchief and held it with its powerful fumes under his nose. "Breathe, Mr. Scott . . . again . . . again . . ."

Under her breath she told Miss Kitty to get a blanket. She did not move the stricken man but covered him where he lay on the floor. Jen and Lucien and Bébé hovered in the doorway. Cherry motioned them to go away, laid her finger on her lips to signify absolute quiet.

"Breathe, Mr. Scott . . ."

The ashen color drained slowly away and Scott's skin looked normal, though very white, again. Cherry wiped away the icy perspiration. She chafed his temples and wrists to stimulate circulation. His breathing was less labored now.

"Pain—" he muttered.

"Don't speak," Cherry said softly. "Rest."

She sat there on the floor with him for twenty or thirty minutes, administering the nitrite once again, keeping closest watch on him. By lying completely still, he seemed to revive. A great relief broke over Cherry as the first trace of normal pink appeared again in his lips.

"Lucien! Bébé!" she called softly.

The two men appeared and Cherry directed them to carry Mr. Scott into his own room. Lucien undressed him and put him to bed. By that time Dr. Pratt had arrived.

The doctor examined the musician and then came out to talk softly with Cherry in the hall.

"He'll be all right."

"I gave him the nitrite, sir."

"Good. Quick work! We might have lost him. Now see here, Cherry. He'll feel perfectly comfortable again after adequate rest. Just try to keep a closer eye on his eating habits, working hours, exertion, to ward off any further attack. Above all, you must *control any emotionally disturbing factors*. Understand?"

"I understand, doctor." Cherry added silently, "But how? How? You don't know, Dr. Pratt, that someone is holding a gun to Scott Owens's head."

Cherry very nearly felt hopeless. She had thought the situation could not be worse, but now—with Scott ill from shock and worry—it had become still darker. For Scott, ill, could not act against Carroll's threat. Scott could not even make the first, simple decision, now.

And, meanwhile, time was on the blackmailer's side.

CHAPTER IX

Night Vigil

WHAT HAPPENED NEXT CAME SO FAST THAT CHERRY lost all track of time.

Had it been two, three, or four days until Scott revived? At any rate, he slept off all traces of the heart attack and in a surprisingly short time insisted he was "as good as new." He seemed to be, and Dr. Pratt agreed that the musician might resume his normal schedule once more.

Scott perversely took this to mean he might go off to give a concert.

"But it's only for one concert," he had pleaded, "only as far as St. Louis, and besides I need every extra cent I can earn, now!"

There was no reasoning with him. It did the musician more harm to hold him back from his music than to let him travel. So once more Scott, Miss Kitty, and

Cherry, laden with music scores, medicines, and the silent keyboard, climbed on a train. Cherry hoped she would see Gwen in St. Louis.

They were just outside of St. Louis, in fact its river and skyscrapers and railroad yards were already in view, when Scott complained of that warning pain in his shoulder. He had an attack on the train. Cherry and Miss Kitty rushed their charge to a hotel and got him into bed.

Cherry immediately summoned the hotel doctor, and telephoned Dr. Pratt long-distance. He gave instructions and referred Cherry to a St. Louis doctor until he himself could get there.

The concert had to be canceled, of course. More than that, a series of concerts for ensuing weeks had to be rescheduled, and many business matters rearranged.

"There's only one way out," Miss Kitty had said. "I'll have to go on alone and see the various concert managers—get them to give me future dates—reorganize the notices and advertising—" She sighed. "The Carroll matter will just have to wait, too. I'm powerless without Scott." She asked Cherry earnestly, "Cherry, do you think you can manage if I leave you here alone with Scott? I'll phone Dr. Pratt to hurry him along. You know what to do in the meantime."

"I can manage. I have this doctor here, and a nurse friend who'll help me, I hope. I'll *have* to manage, Miss Kitty. Mr. Scott must not be moved."

NIGHT VIGIL 145

So Cherry was left alone in a hotel suite with her patient. She immediately telephoned Gwen.

"Of course I'll be your relief nurse!" Gwen said. "I'll come downtown right away!"

Gwen came faithfully every afternoon, to let Cherry snatch a nap or take a walk. The two friends did not manage much visiting, at this rate. Cherry was, most of the time, left alone with Scott Owens.

She was very careful to be circumspect, and not give busybodies the slightest excuse for gossip. She wore her white uniform and regulation white linen cap while nursing in the suite of rooms, but not in the hotel corridor or in the public hotel lobby. That would have been conspicuous and therefore in bad taste. She ate her meals in her own room, not in her patient's room. And whenever a question of personal conduct arose, Cherry asked herself, "How should a nurse behave in order to honor her profession?"

There were plenty of people around to notice whether the nurse bore herself with dignity or not. The presence of this famous musician drew crowds like a magnet: newspapermen—musicians and music lovers—several personal friends—and just curious celebrity hunters. They kept Cherry busy—too busy, taking precious time away from her care of the sick man. She had to protect her patient and herself from these intruders. Yet she dared not offend any of them. She was her patient's personal ambassador, in a way.

Cherry began to realize what extraordinary tact a private duty nurse must exercise. Hastily she worked out a protocol.

To the newspapermen who wanted a daily bulletin on Owens's recovery, Cherry promised to leave word with the desk clerk.

To Scott's personal friends and fellow musicians, Cherry said, "As soon as the doctor gives his permission for our patient to have visitors I'll leave a little flag outside the door, and you may come in. If there's no flag, please don't ring. Because, you see, Mr. Scott would worry if he thought his friends were being turned away. And he insists on an explanation of every sound—who's at the door, who telephoned, and it ruins his rest."

To the idly curious, Cherry said, "Go away!" And she left instructions with the hotel management not to give out the number of Mr. Owens's room.

Cherry faced other difficulties in the actual nursing itself. Accustomed to the facilities of a hospital or at least of a home, here she had nothing to work with except the contents of her small kit and her wits. The hotel bed in which the helpless musician lay was low and broad, so that Cherry had to lean over uncomfortably dozens of times a day. The bathroom was not easy of access. The hotel kitchen sent up elaborate dishes which the patient could not eat.

Cherry summoned up her ingenuity and found what solutions she could. She and Gwen put blocks under

NIGHT VIGIL

the bed, raised it higher, and that put a stop to her backaches. Unfortunately, as Gwen remarked, the location of the bathroom could not be changed, so Cherry had to endure many extra steps, without complaint. She did manage special invalid cookery, using remembered school studies in nutrition and an electric chafing dish which Gwen's aunt contributed.

"It's lonely going," Cherry told the redhead, "left in this impersonal hotel room alone with a sick and sometimes delirious man. Thank goodness, you pop in."

"You have the doctor, the bellboy, and the chambermaid," Gwen dryly pointed out.

"Yes, for about an hour a day. If it weren't for you, I think I'd forget how to speak English!"

Dr. Pratt traveled to see the musician, bringing advice, nursing equipment, and a little more companionship for the stranded nurse. After the doctor left, it was less lonely for Cherry, for Scott Owens began to talk.

But it was vague, rambling talk, mostly about the threat of blackmail which hung over him. Sometimes Scott was delirious and talked mistily of his past.

"He said he'd forgiven me!" he cried out weakly one night. "Matthew said so!"

Matthew, thought Cherry. *Uncle Matthew* who must never be mentioned. What did a dead man have to do with this present trouble?

And once, while Cherry was feeding him, the pianist stared at her with stark eyes and said distinctly, "Prison—a number in prison—that's what it was like—"

And one night he screamed, "The box! The papers in the box in the vault! I *must* have them with me! Go get them for me! I want them with me!"—screamed until Cherry had to hold him down and give him a sedative.

These things unnerved her, particularly at night. One never knew what a delirious patient might try to do—suicide, or attack the nurse, or try to flee. "Such things don't occur often," Gwen reminded her. But she agreed that Cherry had better not go to bed at night, with her patient in such a state. Cherry kept fourteen-, eighteen-, and twenty-hour watches, all through the long nights. She grew very tired.

Daytimes, Scott was more lucid. He talked reasonably, if weakly, about his worries. "I've got to get well and get up and take care of that nasty business," he fretted.

"You won't get well in this frame of mind," Cherry said truthfully. "If you would just stop thinking about it until you are able to cope with it," she urged.

Scott's improvement was very slow. Cherry was troubled for her patient. She tried all the techniques she could think of to soothe him mentally, to help him sleep, to fight back the causes of his delirium.

She also was careful about what *not* to do. Scott's sense of hearing was painfully acute; even when well, his nerves were jumpy. So Cherry did not permit herself to do any annoying shuffling, or clearing her throat, or fussing around the room, or banging, or bumping against his bed. She disciplined herself to the art of sitting perfectly quiet, when not actively at work, reading or mending without making any rustling sounds, without rocking or squeaking in her chair. She avoided continuously, nervously, using her hands. She abandoned a pair of shoes that squeaked for a lighter-weight pair with rubber heels. She kept her voice velvety. Small things, and difficult for a girl bouncing with exuberance, but her efforts at repose were repaid by Scott's quieted nerves.

Cherry also made it her business, as a good nurse, to notice what things annoyed her patient, and shielded him from them. A window shade softly blowing back and forth, the drip of a faucet, a drawer left standing open—such things magnified into annoyances in a sick person's mind. Cherry was quick to correct them before Scott had a chance to become annoyed.

The sick man's day had to be filled somehow, but he was much too ill to read, play cards, or listen for long to the radio. Cherry entertained him by talking with him. She discovered that conversation was still another very important technique of the private duty nurse. She drew on her fund of education, recalled her Army experiences, and wished that she had kept up more on reading. For her patient was a brilliant man, and he demanded that his nurse, who was his constant companion, have a well-stocked mind. Cherry sensed, too, when to let her patient do most of the talking, and when to insist on a complete though friendly silence.

There was also the problem of how to handle this nervous and irritable patient, making him comfortable without continually annoying him with, "Are you comfortable? Do you want a drink of water? Are you warm enough?" Cherry developed a sixth sense about what the invalid wanted, before he himself knew he wanted it. She did not bully Scott into enjoying "his delicious broth" when she had to coax it down spoonful by spoonful. She was pleasant but not infuriatingly cheerful. She avoided ill-timed mirth, and the sort of briskness that would wear out a well person. When Scott began to think he would be more comfortable lying on his other side, Cherry was already turning him, and slipping a fresh, cool pillow under his head.

There was the problem of wakeful, endless nights for Scott, and how to induce sleep. Cherry tried warm drinks before bedtime, a hot-water bottle on Scott's feet. She tried music, via radio, and chose musical selections for what mood each would evoke in her patient.

Cherry could have used some sleep herself. Gwen relieved her only a couple of hours in the afternoon, for she had other duties, and Cherry was growing dangerously tired. Large amounts of black coffee kept her awake through the long night vigils.

Gwen warned her, "You're living on borrowed energy, you'll pay up for this some time in the future."

"Well, if I were in Mr. Owens's own city, I could notify Dr. Pratt that I'm growing overtired and he would secure one or even two full-time relief nurses—nurses whom he knows. But I'm stranded *here*. There's not much I can do, except hide my fatigue from my patient."

One night Scott was sleeping fitfully in the dimly lighted room. Cherry sat at a little distance from the bed. The very sight of pillows and covers made her yawn. Determinedly, she went to the open window and leaned out. She breathed in long, deep draughts of cool night air. It refreshed her.

It was very late. The street below was nearly deserted, electric signs were darkened, there was no traffic. Only street lamps made oases of light in the shadows, only a few solitary footsteps rang out on the empty pavement. Cherry saw a man lurking below their window, on the opposite side of the street.

Half an hour later, she again leaned out the window and again she saw the man. Still there! Why, at this hour? And why was he looking up at their window? He was an inconspicuous man in a dark suit, thoroughly ordinary except that, as the street light fell on his shoulders, Cherry saw that one shoulder was slightly higher than the other. This struck a chord in Cherry's memory.

"It's the man who sat opposite us on the train," she suddenly realized. "That man who was always underfoot. I'm sure it's he!" she told herself. "But why is he trailing us?" In search of a motive for this man's strange behavior, she concentrated on reconstructing every moment of that train ride. Mr. Scott, Miss Kitty, and she had had to ride in Pullman seats, she remembered, and this man, now loitering under the street light, had sat opposite them reading a magazine. But he seemed, Cherry now recalled, to be very much interested in their conversation. What were they discussing? Cherry racked her brains. Oh, yes! The usual thing—fortunetellers. Mr. Scott had heatedly denounced them—especially Gregory Carroll. Carroll—blackmail! The two words suddenly fused with almost physical impact. Cherry grew chill at this sudden realization. "That's it!" she exclaimed excitedly to herself. "That man is trailing Scott Owens—and he must be connected with Carroll!" Panic swept over her.

Cherry impulsively turned to the musician. But he was asleep, and she could not frighten a sick man with this discovery, anyway. She could not telephone Gwen: she had to keep Owens's secret. She had never felt so alone. It was up to her, with her patient helpless, to act—to do whatever must be done. Or perhaps she had no right to act—this was Scott Owens's affair, not hers.

But she was his nurse—his guardian—he lay helpless and she was responsible for protecting him—even protecting him against that man lurking under their window! If a patient was too ill to think or act, in time of emergency, then his nurse must do it for him! A shiver went down Cherry's back. At the same moment,

NIGHT VIGIL

the words of the nurses' pledge flashed through her mind and steadied her.

"Maybe I'm imagining things about that man in the street! Or maybe I'm half asleep and dreaming the whole thing!"

She went into her own adjoining room where no lights were on and looked out the window from there. No, she was not imagining it. There the man stood, only now he had furtively stepped back deeper into shadow.

With hands that shook, Cherry picked up her telephone and whispered into it:

"Please send a policeman up to Room 302."

She returned to Scott, in 304, to wait. What exactly did she fear the man might do? She did not know. He might only be following them to secure information, or to prevent the blackmailer's potential victim from slipping away. Or—he might try some violence. It would be easy—a sick man and a female nurse. That man was powerfully built. Cherry was badly scared.

She heard a tap on the door of 302 and ran in there, and opened it. A policeman stood there in the sleeping hotel corridor. Cherry took one reassuring look at the huge bulk of him in his blue coat, at his badge which spelled "law." With him was a hotel clerk, anxiety in his pale face.

"What's wrong, miss?" the officer asked.

Cherry explained in a low voice. "And I *do* recognize him. He's trailing us, I'm positive of it!"

The policeman said calmly, "Maybe he's just a loiterer. I'll go down and talk to him."

Cherry hurried back to the window. Yes, the man was still there—she had been afraid the sight of a policeman might frighten him away. A minute passed. Then she saw the policeman come out of the hotel, alone. He crossed the street leisurely, swinging his night stick, his footsteps echoing in the night air. The loiterer did not budge. The policeman went up to him. They both stood under the street lamp in full sight.

Cherry could hear their two voices, but not the words. They talked for a few minutes. Then the man pulled a wallet out of his pocket, showed some papers to the policeman. To Cherry's horror, the policeman nodded, turned, and retraced his steps back to the hotel. The man continued to stand there. Cherry thought or imagined she saw him smile.

Again there was a tap on the door of 302.

"You're mistaken, miss!" The policeman grinned down at her and his expression said plainly: "Just another hysterical female."

"But what—he's trailing us, I tell you—"

"Sure he is. He's hired to do that. He's a private detective lookin' out for the two of you. A bodyguard. Mr. Owens hired him himself."

"It's the first I heard of it! I—I don't believe it."

"He showed me written proof, miss."

NIGHT VIGIL 155

"But I don't believe— Officer, you're mistaken! You've *got* to help me— Let me explain—"

"Now, now, what're you trying to do? You could have caused a false arrest! That's plenty serious. You take my word for it and go to bed. Everything's in order!"

He tipped his hat and strolled away, leaving her shaken, on realizing that she could not turn to the police for help.

A private detective? A bodyguard? Cherry puzzled over it. She did not know what to think. The celebrity had hired him himself?—yet had never told her? And why should he have told her? There was no possibility of discussing such a thing with the sick man. Cherry remained undecided, and disturbed, about the whole incident.

Less than a week later, Scott Owens had improved enough to be able to travel. Cherry said a reluctant goodbye to Gwen Jones. Lucien came to St. Louis, and he and Cherry got the musician on the train, and took him home.

CHAPTER X

A Wig, A Lure, A Lie

CHERRY, UNABLE NOW TO GO TO THE POLICE, WENT sleuthing on her own.

Miss Kitty still was out of town. Cherry was secretly grateful for this as Miss Kitty would have confused the situation much more. She was grateful, too, that there were Dr. Pratt, Jen, and Bébé to help look after the ill musician. Besides, Dr. Pratt urged the overworked nurse to get outdoors, to take the day off. Cherry had been impatiently waiting for this chance. She dressed carefully, put ample money in her purse, and left the Owens house without saying where she was going. Her plan was not clear: she only felt somehow that she needed more information, needed some lead as how Carroll might strike next.

She headed straight for the expensive neighborhood and apartment building where Gregory Carroll had his headquarters.

But it was not so easy to get upstairs. The doorman stopped her as she was halfway through the lobby.

"Whom do you wish to see, miss?"

"Oh, it's all right. I'm expected."

"Sorry, miss, but we have to announce all callers. The management doesn't let anyone go upstairs unless we call up the tenant you want to see on the house phone."

"But I have an appointment, they're expecting me," Cherry bluffed.

The doorman was adamant. "Whom do you wish to see, miss?" He picked up the house telephone. "Who shall I say is calling?"

Cherry sighed. "Miss Ames to see Mr. Gregory Carroll." Carroll would never agree to see her, she thought. It would never do to forewarn him.

"Mr. Carroll?" the doorman repeated. "Mr. Carroll has moved away, or at least he's gone away temporarily. Isn't that right, Bill?" he said to the elevator man.

"That's right."

"His secretary, then," Cherry said stubbornly.

"Mr. Thatch is gone too, miss."

Cherry had not expected this development. But she was not going to be routed so easily. Maybe Carroll had instructed the doorman to say "Not at home."

"Then I'd like to see the superintendent, please." Cherry sat herself down on one of the lobby chairs and unhurriedly took out her compact and powdered her nose, to show that she really intended to stay and see the superintendent.

In about five minutes a stocky, middle-aged man in a navy blue suit came out of a corridor behind the elevator.

"I'm Mr. Bixby, the superintendent." He looked at her doubtfully. Part of his job was to see that the tenants' privacy was protected, and he did not like intruders. Cherry at once put on her most feminine and helpless air.

"Oh, Mr. Bixby, I'm sorry to bother you, I know I'm being a nuisance, but I just have to see Mr. Carroll. Please?"

"I'm sorry, miss, but Mr. Carroll has gone away. There's nobody up there now."

"Oh, dear. When will he be back?"

"I don't know, miss."

"Did he leave a forwarding address?"

"You can leave all messages here and they will be picked up."

"You mean he's moved away? Because if he has, I—ah—might be interested in subleasing his apartment." That should pry the information out of him. He would want to sublease an apartment if it were vacant.

A WIG, A LURE, A LIE 159

"I couldn't say if he's moved away, or just gone temporarily, miss. You'd have to ask our renting office. I can give you the address—it's downtown."

Cherry was stumped. But somehow she did not believe the superintendent. He would know whether or not there was an apartment for rent or for sublease in his own building. He was lying. Possibly his discreet evasiveness had been purchased by a large tip from Carroll. Well, she had money in her purse, too. Cherry had scruples against bribes and against lying. But when fighting against such people as these blackmailers, she had no choice. Either she could go through with this, or passively let Scott Owens get hurt! Coaxingly she said:

"Mr. Bixby, I'll tell you what's really on my mind. I'm in the silliest jam—I'm one of Mr. Carroll's regular clients, you've probably seen me here before. And the last time I was here"—she thought fast—if only she could get into that apartment, she might learn something!—"I left my furs. Stupidly went off and left my furs! In Mr. Carroll's private study."

"Mm-hmm." The superintendent seemed to believe her. He was used to Mr. Carroll's women clients.

"So if you could *please* let me in there—" She delicately pressed a folded bill into his hand. His fingers curled over it. "I'd be so grateful, Mr. Bixby."

"I could take you in there myself for a few minutes, while we look for your furs."

"Thank you so much! That will be a great help!"

"Just wait till I get the keys."

He came back with a bunch of keys and took one off the key ring.

Upstairs Mr. Bixby opened the door to Carroll's apartment, admitted Cherry, and followed her in. The beautiful, stagy room was just as she remembered it, with a pall of silence hanging over it now—no, there was something different! Cherry's darting dark eyes, alert for anything she could learn up here, noted that the harpsichord was gone. Scott's shrewd guess that the fortunetellers had rented the harpsichord to impress him was right!

Cherry fussed around the big room, pretending to look for her imaginary furs. She particularly hung around Mr. Thatch's desk. It was not littered any longer; there was nothing on it to supply her with fresh leads.

The superintendent said warningly, "You said you left your furs in Mr. Carroll's study?"

"Yes."

Cherry went on into the little room and poked around, her eyes never leaving his desk. Nothing here, either. She dared not open the desk drawers. Mr. Bixby was watching her. She straightened up and sighed.

"My furs aren't here. I guess Mr. Carroll has taken them along with him for safekeeping and will return them to me." It was the best she could say, to save her face.

"Were the furs valuable?" the superintendent asked.

"Quite valuable. But I'm sure I left them here, and Mr. Carroll's so nice, I know he'll take care of them, so I won't worry too much. If only I knew where to reach him"—Cherry tentatively tried again for information—"I'm going away and will need my furs—"

He did not answer. He went to the entrance door and held it open for Cherry. She walked through, defeated.

But downstairs in the lobby, on the table, lay a pile of mail for the mailman—the letters which tenants of the building wanted mailed. Pushed to one side was a letter already postmarked and marked in pencil: *Please Forward.* That letter was addressed to Carroll! The superintendent must have marked it! Hastily Cherry read and memorized:

Please forward to:
c/o James Smith
   412 Huneker Street, City

Huneker Street was a shabby residential street, and Number 412 was an old brownstone house converted into apartments.

Cherry stood in the small vestibule and studied the names over the brass letter boxes and bells. There was no Carroll or Smith or Thatch listed. Some of the name brackets were left empty. Cherry tried the heavy door into the building, then jiggled the doorknob. It was locked. She rang the bell marked *Superintendent*.

The buzzer on the door buzzed and released the lock. Cherry opened and went in. A stout, pleasant woman in a housedress came out of the first apartment.

"You looking for the superintendent?"

"Yes, I am. Could you help me locate Mr. Carroll?"

The woman looked puzzled. "We have no one named Carroll here."

"He's in care of Mr. James Smith, I believe."

"Smith? Smith? What does he look like, dearie?"

Cherry hesitated. Then she described Gregory Carroll "—and medium height, a very serious, almost saintly expression. Remarkable blue eyes, and blonde hair."

"Aha! I know the very one you mean." The woman closed her own door and stepped out into the hall. "Very saintly looking, he is. You'd notice him any place. Only you're mistaken about his hair, dearie. He has *red* hair. A regular mop of it."

"Red hair?" Cherry echoed.

"Beautiful red hair," the stout woman declared. "I'd be happy to have it on me own head."

Cherry kept the woman chatting while she tried to figure out a further angle. "His name wasn't Carroll, you say? I must be all mixed up."

"No, indeed. His name was Lawrence. John Alter Lawrence. I remember because it's such a beautiful, high-sounding name."

Was this redheaded Lawrence the same man as Gregory Carroll or not? Cherry said tentatively, "He usually is with an elderly man—looks like a teacher."

A WIG, A LURE, A LIE 163

The woman nodded emphatically. "I know the one, the very one. Looks like a dried-up leaf, don't he? Always with Mr. Lawrence. I supposed he was his brother, though they don't look alike, but *some* brothers—"

She had located Carroll and Mr. Thatch, then! They did live here!

"Ah, no, they aren't here any more," the woman said. "What a shame, dearie. They moved out only day before yesterday. See, they had the apartment next to mine, sublet it furnished. It's empty now, see?"

She went down the hall a few paces, Cherry following her, and swung open an unlocked door. Cherry went in, and looked around at the dark, meagerly furnished rooms. There was nothing there, not a trace.

"Did they leave a forwarding address?" Cherry asked.

"That they didn't. They were here only a bit over a week." The woman chatted on, about her troubles with transients.

Cherry thanked her, and was going down the front steps, when the woman called after her:

"The third one was named Fuller, if I remember rightly. Yes, dearie, a Mr. Fuller. But no Smith, no Carroll."

"Well, thank you very much indeed."

A third one! So there was no James Smith but there *was* a third confederate!

Cherry wandered down the street, found a stationery store which had a small soda fountain, ordered a Coke, and sat down to think.

That she had traced the two men this far, and uncovered the existence of a third man working with them, she had no doubt. She was on the right track. But why were they moving around like this? Why using assumed names? To keep out of sight, obviously—Perhaps the police were looking for them on another charge. Cherry's heart rose at that possibility. If Carroll were already in trouble, that might make things easier for Scott Owens!

"That would be too good to be true," Cherry thought. She sipped her Coke. "Besides, Carroll is a shrewd operator. Even if he is in trouble, he'll wiggle out of it. And trouble wouldn't hamper him from striking at Mr. Scott anyway. They could use extra money now. No," she decided, "to be on the safe side, I'll throw out the optimism and look at the worst possibilities."

Why were they moving around like this? In self-defense? To dodge aggressive blows from somebody—maybe they were dodging Cherry herself! She recalled how Carroll, in telling her "fortune," had warned her not to meddle in affairs not her own. "You won't help them—you will only bring trouble, for them and for yourself," he had said. That was the day he had predicted trouble for Scott, too. Quite a "prediction," Cherry thought ironically, when Carroll intended to

A WIG, A LURE, A LIE 165

make the trouble come true via his own blackmail! He certainly had given them broad hints—he had wanted to be "helpful"!

Why were they moving around like this? What other possible reasons were there? Because being in hiding facilitated the working out of some scheme of theirs—or, because they wanted to meet the third confederate away from their apartment where he would be observed, or—But how important was it to know this, anyway? It could be for any of a dozen reasons. Cherry realized she could go on fruitlessly speculating for hours. The only way she could secure definite information was to get back on their trail again.

How was she to find Carroll? And what about that red hair?

"A wig!" Cherry exclaimed out loud.

"Huh?" said the soda jerk. "Another Coke?"

Cherry sputtered and choked on her drink. "Yes, yes, another Coke." But she left it sitting. "Have you a telephone directory? A classified one?"

The boy inclined his head. "Over near the phone booth, in back."

Cherry hastily thumbed to the W's. Watches ... weavers ... welding ... wigmakers. There were ten wigmakers in this city. She wrote down the ten names and addresses.

F. Mittelhopf had a big plate-glass window, a small second-floor shop in the theatrical section. He was a gnarled little man in a black apron. Standing around the shop were faceless plaster heads wearing various wigs—a man's powdered Colonial peruke, with pigtail and black ribbon—flowing golden braids—even a head of green hair.

"No, red hairs for man I do not make," said F. Mittelhopf. "For the theater, I make. See the green one—for the *première danseuse* in the ballet, she is ladyfish—mermaid. For man everyday, I do not make."

Georges *et* Dorothea turned out to be a beauty salon. The stylish woman assistant was busy and crisp. "We make only transformations for women. Sorry."

Mr. Oscar was in the theatrical district too but his window bore in small gold letters: "Wigs—Toupees—Transformations—For Street Wear." Cherry went in. Mr. Oscar was a young man who first demanded of Cherry:

"Sell me your hair! It's magnificent!"

"I—I need it myself," Cherry faltered. "Did you make a—"

"Black curls! Black! I'll give you a good price."

"No!" Cherry shouted back. "Please tell me if you made a red wig for a man."

"My father did make a red wig, last year. Wait. I'll look it up in my books."

Cherry sat down and glanced around the strange shop. The man came back beaming. "Here it is. A red wig for Mrs. J. F. Thornton, 1474 Columbus Drive, shoulder length bob, with an additional chignon for evening wear."

"No, that's not it," Cherry said wearily. "Thank you.— No! I *won't* sell you my curls!"

She escaped in a hurry, laughing despite her disappointment.

Wigmakers four, five, six, and seven were also disappointments. The eighth looked more promising. "Effanjay's Wig Company—Street Wear—Costume Wigs—Wigs for Dolls—Custom-Made and Rental." Rental! Cherry went in.

"Yes, young lady, we rented a red wig to a man two weeks ago. But why do you want to know?"

Cherry smiled mischievously. "Because the man is my uncle and I want to play a joke on him. Only I haven't his current address." She hoped that by not asking the man's name, she would sound convincing. It worked. The wigmaker opened his books.

"79 Merriam Avenue."

"Thank you!"

Cherry flounced out, encouraged once more. Too bad she could not get the name, too, but the address was the thing. She was lucky to get it.

79 Merriam Avenue was a private frame house in the suburbs. Cherry strolled along the opposite side of the street, looking at it, hoping she was unobtrusive. It was

just a gray house with a hedge in front of it, a flight of steps to the stoop. It stood between two other houses, their small lawns adjoining without fences. A window shade in one of 79's second-story windows was pulled up as she watched. Someone was home. No car parked out in front. No dog. Cherry strolled around the block several times, wondering if she really dared go up and ring the doorbell.

Finally she screwed up all her courage and started to cross the street. Her heart thumped wildly. Was anyone watching her from those curtained windows? She did not venture to look up. What was she going to find in there? What danger was she deliberately walking into? Yet her feet carried her forward and her eyes looked ahead to the doorbell.

She was almost across the street when a man in shirt sleeves came limping from the back yard—but whether from the back yard of 79 or 77 Merriam Avenue, it was impossible to tell. He limped badly and was groaning. He almost stumbled into Cherry.

"Oh-h—excuse me, miss! Ugh, my ankle!"

Instantly her nurse's instincts were alert. "Have you hurt yourself? Let's see."

The man extended a stiff ankle. "—working in my garage—fell and twisted my ankle—no one's home—I've got to"—he said painfully—"get to the corner drugstore. Get Doc to look at this for me, if he's in. At least get some liniment. Oh-h!"

"I'll go get the liniment for you," Cherry said. "I'm a nurse and I'll look at your ankle for you. Which is your house?"

He pointed to Number 79. That was a stroke of luck! Now she could get in without having to force or talk her way in!

"Well, get in the house," Cherry said. "I'll be right in, with some liniment."

He dug in his pants pocket. "Here's a dollar for it. You're awfully kind."

"Not at all." She sped away, after first seeing that the man slowly limped into Number 79.

In five minutes she was back with the liniment and heavy gauze—five minutes too late. A car with three men in it was just turning the corner at the far end of the block. And 79 Merriam Avenue, doors and windows locked, stood deserted.

CHAPTER XI

Nocturnal Visitor

CHERRY COULD GUESS ONLY TOO VIVIDLY WHAT THE consequences of her wild-goose chase might be. Her action had warned the blackmailing fortuneteller that Owens or his nurse was trying to fight back. Now he would strike in earnest—strike hard, and soon.

Cherry was sick with remorse at the way she had fumbled things and given her plans away. Whatever now befell Scott Owens, she would have accelerated it. She decided she must be extra careful, take every possible precaution—and make Mr. Scott do the same—to forestall any next step by Carroll and his gang.

But the musician insisted on a most foolish and reckless step.

The pianist was still ill and worrying. He was quite unreasonable in what he demanded, and that unreasonableness was a symptom of his illness. His nurse tried to point out to him that he was not thinking clearly. But to no avail: the impractical, oversensitive artist was never a very sensible being, even when well.

"No, you've got to do it for me, Cherry!" he insisted from his bed. "I want those papers—the proof—with me. Here. Right here in the house."

"But they won't be safe here," Cherry pleaded. "And they are safe in the bank vault."

"The papers will be perfectly all right at home. I have a wall safe here in my room."

"A wall safe isn't any too secure."

"Yes, it is," Scott insisted stubbornly. "The only reason I use a bank vault is because I'm away traveling so much, and don't like to leave papers lying about in an empty house."

"Please, please, Mr. Scott, leave the papers where they are! What do you want them for, anyhow? You can't do anything much with them, you said."

"Never mind that. I simply want them *here*. If I can touch them, see them, I'll feel a lot better."

He fretted so, and wore himself out with such worrying that after two or three days of useless argument, Cherry gave in. She agreed to go to the bank vault, get the precious papers of proof—she still did not know what they proved or disproved—and bring them home to Mr. Scott.

First, he instructed her to write a letter of explanation to Miss Kitty, and ask her to send the vault key and a written power of attorney to open the safety deposit box. He himself did not have this. Without these, Cherry could not have touched the box. She wrote as Scott Owens demanded. Two more days passed while awaiting a reply. Two anxious days during which Cherry tried yet again to get her patient to abandon his foolish plan. He would not be moved. Then Miss Kitty's letter came, with the key enclosed.

"Now you'll open the bank vault," Scott Owens said.

"Please, no, Mr. Scott—"

"You must go—I'll get out of bed and go myself—"

"All right, I'll do as you say," Cherry said, heavy with misgivings.

Scott's thin face looked happy. "It's documentary evidence of my innocence, don't you see?"

"All the more reason it should be left in a safe place—at a time like this!"

But she had no choice. She went downtown to the bank.

The vault was reached by going down a flight of marble stairs, deep into the basement of the bank. Cherry followed an airless, electrically lighted corridor, protected by iron bars, and came to a locked, iron-bar door, like a prison door. An armed bank guard on the inside, gun in its holster on his hip, unlocked the door and admitted her. Cherry looked around. She had never been in one of these safety deposit vaults before, although almost every bank has one. She was in a storeroom of vast wealth.

This was a sort of noiseless subterranean office, with two men working at desks, fans and electric lights going. Five or six more uniformed, armed bank guards were ranged quietly along the room and in an inside room. A kind of mammoth safe, its thick round steel door standing open, its complicated time lock exposed, comprised a circular entrance into that next room, which was the vault itself. The whole second room seemed to be a giant safe.

"Yes?" One of the men at the desks looked up at Cherry.

"I wish to open the vault rented by Mr. Scott and Miss Kitty Owens. Here is the key, and power of attorney signed by Miss Owens, made out to me. And here is identification of who I am." Cherry produced a letter addressed to her, and her own savings bankbook.

"Hmm." The bank official examined them all very carefully. "Have you any further identification?"

"My Nurses' Association card." Cherry opened her purse and showed this too.

The man beckoned her to a small counter. While she waited, he pulled out a file, extracted a card with Miss Kitty's signature, compared it to the signature on the power of attorney she had sent Cherry. Then he asked Cherry to sign her name and compared it with her signature on her nurse's card. Satisfied, he finally permitted her to sign an authorization to open the Owens's vault box, then he countersigned the authorization, then he stamped it in a bank machine, and at last handed it to her.

"Now, this admits you into the vault. Show this to one of the guards in there."

"Gosh," Cherry thought, "they certainly are careful. This is a regular arsenal."

She stepped over the round, thick, steel rim into the vault itself, and found herself in an amazing room. Its walls were lined with hundreds of locked steel drawers, identified only by engraved numbers. Some of the drawers, or safety deposit boxes, were small, some deeper, some enormous. Four armed guards stood about this inside room. It could, Cherry saw, be closed off with an emergency gate. There was an emergency telephone in here, too. A few desks and chairs were placed in the center of this vault. At one of them, a man was sorting business papers. It was very quiet, except for the hum of fans. The electric lights threw a powerful glare into every possible corner.

A gray-haired guard was grinning at Cherry. "Haven't you ever seen a vault before, young lady?"

"No, I haven't. What's in these boxes, anyhow?" Cherry asked curiously.

"Mostly people's papers brought here for safekeeping—stocks and bonds, business contracts, insurance policies, wills, deeds to property, mortgages. But in some of those great big boxes there are valuable paintings, and gold and silver art objects. And there're enough diamonds locked in these walls to ransom a king."

Cherry was breathless. In one way this place looked only businesslike and rather grim, just rows of shining gray steel drawers. But it held enough drama, Cherry realized, enough potential fireworks for many, many people's lives to—She cut short her imaginings and said, "May I have my box, please?" and handed the guard the key, with its tag bearing the number 14303.

The guard took her key and authorization slip, went down the rows of drawers, found 14303, unlocked it with the Owens's key and then with an additional key which was chained to his belt. He slid the box out of its slot in the wall and brought it back to Cherry at one of the desks. She sat down and examined it. It was a very long, narrow, shallow, black metal box with a hinged lid.

Lifting the lid, she found it crammed with papers. There was also a red tooled-leather jewel box, locked, which Cherry passed over. Mr. Scott had said the papers he wanted were in a long blue envelope. Here it was! It was not sealed. Cherry was bursting with curiosity but she had no right to look at Mr. Owens's confidential papers, and she did not. She put the blue envelope in her purse and tucked her purse tight against her side. The guard returned the box to its place in the wall safe, locked it in, and handed Cherry back her key. She walked out through the two rooms, and the heavy iron outer gate swung shut and locked again behind her.

It was only when she had climbed up the stairs and out onto the busy street that Cherry wondered if anyone could have been following her. She had no reason to think so—she had seen nothing, heard nothing untoward. But a faint prick of uneasiness needled her mind. A sort of animal instinct in her had been awakened, and she felt sure someone had been looking at her.

"I'm just being apprehensive," she decided. "All I have to worry about is getting off this crowded street and home with these irreplaceable papers, as fast as I can!"

At home her patient was awaiting her, eager and bright-eyed. He put the blue envelope under his pillow.

"For goodness' sake, Mr. Scott, don't leave those papers *under your pillow*! Find a safer place!"

"Where? Inside my piano scores? In Kit's desk? Oh, of course. There's a wall safe here in my room—I'll put them in right away— Why, Bébé! Hello! Come in, come in. I was wishing for visitors."

Cherry bent over her patient and gently reminded him, "Mr. Scott, put the envelope away right now while we're both thinking of it!"

NOCTURNAL VISITOR 177

Scott asked Bébé and Cherry to go outside in the hall. They waited a few minutes, until Scott called.

"Bébé, sit down," he said lightheartedly. Scott seemed happier than in days, now that he had the papers with him. "No, not on that chair. On the big one."

"That chair and me," said the fat man, "is like Joe Spratt and his grandmother, no?"

"No!" Scott laughed. "You mean Jack Spratt and his—"

"Don't told me already. I mean Humpty Plumpty and the Hi Diddle Doodle, no?"

Scott's laughter rang out. "Bébé's setting Mother Goose to music— Cherry, where are you going?"

"Nowhere. Just to my room. I—I'm a little tired."

She was not so much tired as depressed about the presence of those papers. Later, again, she protested to Scott. But the sick man would not give them up. "I want the papers here, to show the press, just in case. But I do admit, Cherry, that Carroll would certainly like to have these papers in his possession. If he could get hold of them, the extortion would start at once."

"Then why—why—" Cherry exhorted. But still he would not surrender them. Cherry wondered again what they told and what Mr. Scott was hiding.

"Nothing can happen!" he scoffed as Cherry made him comfortable for the night. "Jen and Lucien are right downstairs, and Lucien's a light sleeper. We have three yapping poodles. And you're on the same floor with me now." For, in Miss Kitty's absence and during Scott's slow rest and recovery, Cherry had moved down a floor. She now temporarily occupied Miss Kitty's bedroom, directly across the hall from Mr. Scott's sleeping room.

"Well, at least we'll take the precaution of using the bell," Cherry said stubbornly.

Cherry referred to an arrangement she used now that Mr. Scott was no longer so ill. She had stopped her exhausting, all-night watching, and now went to bed and to sleep herself. Ordinarily a nurse would awaken at the sound of her own name. But Cherry was not certain of hearing a faint call from the patient's bedroom. Therefore she had bought a small hand bell, tied a long cord to it, fastened the end of the cord to Mr. Scott's bed, and nightly she placed the bell on the edge of a chair beside her own bed. A tug on the cord by Mr. Scott, and the bell tumbled down, making enough clatter to thoroughly arouse her. Scott Owens did not ring often, only once or twice so far.

The bell beside Cherry's bed rang that night. Cherry awoke with a start. She groped for her robe, thinking it must be very late, and started to climb drowsily out of bed. Then she saw a figure in the hall, silhouetted between her open door and Mr. Scott's open door, caught in the faint street light diffused from Scott's windows. She was suddenly wide awake. Her patient had gotten out of bed!—she was horrified—she must get him right back into bed. Quickly she snapped on the lights, and choked back the screams rising in her throat. For it was not Scott Owens. It was a powerfully built man whose left shoulder was noticeably higher than his right one. He ran soundlessly down the stairs.

She heard the front door close, then heard the motor of a car. She ran into Mr. Scott's room, leaned out the window, saw nothing. She turned on a lamp and ran to her patient. He was asleep. He awakened uneasily and blinked at her.

"What's the matter?" he yawned.

Cherry apologetically told him she thought she had heard him call out for the papers hidden in the wall safe, and hastily added that she must have been dreaming.

Scott laughed sleepily and scoffingly told her not to worry about them—they were perfectly safe and he directed her to the wall safe to check it. To her great relief, she found that the safe was closed tight. It had held fast against the thief's efforts! The papers were still untouched.

But if the Carroll gang had been bold enough *to break into their victim's house*— They surely were going to strike now!

Quickly Cherry settled her patient for the night and went back to her own room. She stumbled over Do, Re, and Mi, fast asleep on the stair landing.

CHAPTER XII

Miss Ames Is "Detained"

ALL THAT SLEEPLESS NIGHT, CHERRY EXAMINED HER conscience. It was a conscience that ached and reproached her. She felt it was partly her fault that the thug had broken in, for Mr. Scott's papers of proof were here and she had brought them here. And she still felt it was her duty to take action for her helpless patient, in his behalf and for his protection. Miss Kitty was still out of town: there was not another soul besides Cherry who knew Scott Owens was in trouble: only Cherry remained to help him.

By morning she had come to a decision. She remained quietly in her own room to think things out. Carroll would strike soon. She could not delay action any longer. She could not go to the police for help. The only thing left was to smoke out Carroll and try to learn *how* he would strike. Forewarned, Scott might be forearmed. She was going out after Carroll. By any means that came to hand.

If her methods had to be questionable, at least her motives were beyond reproach. And if she were walking straight into danger—well, she was in a dangerous spot already. Cherry was desperate enough to try almost anything.

Her plan was logical and to the point. She reached it by tracing back all she had learned, and then putting together what she knew. The man who had broken in last night was the same man who had eavesdropped on the train, who had trailed them in St. Louis. He was obviously connected with Carroll. He had wanted the papers for Carroll. He would have to report back to Carroll. Where? Not to 79 Merriam Avenue, because the blackmailers knew Cherry was watching that address. Not to the Huneker Street place, either, because the talkative woman superintendent would surely tell them Cherry had been seeking them there. To some brand-new address? Possibly. Or—let's see—Cherry tried to imagine herself in their place—it would be simpler for them to go some place already established. Like the big, expensive apartment. They undoubtedly believed, and could verify from Mr. Bixby, that Cherry thought the big headquarters apartment stood empty.

"That's it!" Cherry snapped her fingers. "They'll gamble on my having checked that place already, and having given it up! Now, how to get in there?"

A substantial tip to Mr. Bixby, the superintendent, to admit her to the apartment? No, it might not work. Suppose Carroll had returned—then Bixby would tell Carroll about Cherry's tip, forewarning him. Suppose Carroll actually was in the apartment? All right, she would ring the doorbell and simply walk in, or try to. Or, if he were not there—if the apartment was really vacant—? Then Cherry would have to get in on her own, somehow. And what time should she go? This morning? This afternoon? Cherry decided on the afternoon. She needed a little more time to think, a little more courage.

It was about one o'clock when Cherry dressed in entirely different clothes than she had worn on her last sleuthing expedition, hoping to be less recognizable, and left the Owens house. Once again she went to the expensive neighborhood and Carroll's apartment building, but this time she stopped off on the way to purchase a large bouquet of flowers.

The doorman stopped her, as she had expected.

"I have to deliver these flowers to Apartment 9B," Cherry said, shielding her face behind the bouquet.

The doorman did not remember her from the other day. He merely said, "Use the service elevator," and waved her ahead.

Cherry discovered a second elevator and its operator, and also the stairs every apartment building must have in case of fire. She rode up on the service elevator to the ninth floor. She pretended, for the

MISS AMES IS "DETAINED" 183

elevator operator's benefit, to head toward 9B, but once the service elevator had gone down, she tucked the bouquet in a corner of the stairway.

She was on the floor below Carroll's. She simply did not have the courage to go up, ring Carroll's doorbell, and possibly come face to face with him or Mr. Thatch. Besides, they might not let her in. She *had* to get in some other way, without their knowing. But how?

Cherry listened. She heard no voices or footsteps. Good, the coast was clear. She slipped out into the corridor and her eye fell on the door of 9A—directly under Carroll's apartment which was 10A. The door of 9A stood slightly ajar. Cherry tiptoed over to it, peeked in, and rejoiced.

The apartment under Carroll's was empty of furniture and was in the process of being painted. Paint buckets, ladders, and canvases were strewn about the empty rooms. All the doors and windows had been left open, no doubt for circulation to dispel the paint odor. Best of all, the painters were nowhere in sight—gone on their lunch hour. Here was a piece of luck!

Cherry darted across the empty, paint-spattered living room and climbed out the window onto the fire escape. She quickly walked up one flight, praying no one would notice and report her on these outside iron stairs, praying that Carroll's fire-escape window might be unlocked.

It was. A little tugging opened it. Cherry slipped over the window sill, her heart banging away in both guilt and exultation, and carefully closed the window behind her. She stood at last in Carroll's elaborate living room. The apartment was still, dusty, hot from being unaired.

But she stood there only a split second, for she heard the elevator door clang open and then close on this floor, and several voices and footsteps in the hall. Cherry fled to the big couch and crouched behind it. Perhaps the people in the hall would head for another apartment than Carroll's. She hoped so, for she wanted a chance to search his place. But even as she strained her ears for the direction of the footsteps, a key turned in the door.

Instantly Cherry dropped completely out of sight behind the sofa.

Footsteps—men's voices— How many people had come in? *Who* had come in? Cherry listened hard, scarcely breathing. She wanted to get out at once. But she was trapped. She had to stay now.

"Open the windows, for heaven's sake!" That was Carroll. Carroll himself! Cherry trembled.

She heard the sound of windows being pushed up, and then the traffic noises.

"I'll go get the papers out of the file on this case." That pedantic voice belonged to Mr. Thatch.

"For our council of war, huh?" A man speaking, a rough voice—who was he?

"Council of war thanks to you, you idiot," Carroll said. "Papers right there in the wall safe, and you muffed it! You failed to get the most important thing!"

"Well, *I* wouldn't mind a drink." This was a woman's voice and it sounded vaguely familiar. Someone sat down heavily on the sofa. Cherry fearfully looked up. She beheld tarnished blonde hair, a fat pink neck, a lace collar—why, it was Mrs. Crawford! The clairvoyant from Bluewater!

"I certainly am going to learn things today!" Cherry exulted even in the midst of her panic. "Even if I am trapped in here— Oh, Lordy, I hope they don't find me! At least I hope they don't find me before I hear enough! Maybe—maybe they'll all leave together, as they came, or most of them anyhow, and then I can slip out unnoticed. I *hope!*"

"Come on, come on," said still another man's voice, and Cherry half-recognized this voice too. "Can't we start the extortion even without the papers? When are you going to tell me the whole story? After all, I've put up the money for this job, I've got a right to know exactly how you work."

"Certainly, certainly, Mercer," Carroll replied smoothly.

Now she placed that voice! It belonged to the man who had limped out from in back of 79 Merriam Avenue and said he had sprained his ankle! The third confederate! Carroll—Mr. Thatch—this Mercer—Mrs.

Crawford—And the fifth? Cherry lay flat on her stomach and peeked around the sofa leg. The fifth man was the man whose left shoulder was higher than his right one. Mr. Thatch was addressing him as Joe.

Cherry pulled her head back turtle fashion and lay down quietly to listen. She was so fascinated that her fear died down a little. The footsteps ceased, chairs creaked, papers rattled. Cherry smelled cigarette smoke. Apparently the five had sat down and settled themselves to talk.

"All right, tell me," demanded the man called Mercer. "Now that we're finally in a safe place, and all together, tell me exactly how you operate."

"It is absurdly simple," said Mr. Thatch, amusement in his precise voice. "We prefer it to laboring for a livelihood. We've really let you in on a very good thing, Mr. Mercer."

"Shut up, Thatch, I'm head man here," said Carroll. There was a prickly silence. "Mercer, you won't regret your investment—you'll quadruple your money. You're just lucky that we needed ready money in a hurry and I had to take you in. But since you've bought your way in, I'll tell you how we work it."

Cherry literally held her breath, so as not to miss a syllable.

"We are a ring of fortunetellers," Carroll explained, "and we operate throughout cities and towns and villages all over the country. We must have three, four hundred fortunetellers— How many, Thatch?"

"Nearly four hundred."

"—nearly four hundred so-called fortunetellers working under my direction. All the fortunetelling we do, you can stick in your eye. We run an extortion racket. We get confidential personal information about some sucker—some information he'd rather keep quiet—and then we threaten to expose him, and demand hush money."

Mercer asked curiously, "How do you get hold of such secret personal information?"

"In several ways, and we're experts at all of them." Mrs. Crawford let out a shrill laugh at this. Carroll said, "Quiet, Mamie! The easiest way to get information is from the 'client' himself—or herself, they're mostly women."

"I don't get it," Mercer said. "You mean people deliberately give away their secrets?"

"Not deliberately," said Carroll. "We pump it out of 'em—or scare it out of 'em—in the course of telling their fortunes. We can get a person so upset that she doesn't realize she is talking too much."

"And then there are my methods." This was Mr. Thatch's dry voice. "I make polite conversation with the clients while they're waiting to see The Master. People trust a quiet, elderly man. Owens's sister was invaluable, she talked her head off to me—in strict confidence, of course. I also chat with clients' relatives, chauffeurs, delivery boys, friends, and business associates. Just a little innocent gossip—a little from this one, a little from that one, it adds up—then I turn the whole story over to Mr. Carroll. Then he goes to work."

Carroll said crossly, "You spend enough of our money on telegrams and cables."

Mr. Thatch said apologetically, "You want me to check up on every rumor I hear that could do us any good, don't you? Besides, Mr. Mercer, I am a great newspaper reader—current papers and old ones. In fact, it was while I was going through a file of newspapers from twenty years ago that I dug up the information about Scott Owens."

"And it was me who saw in the newspaper," put in Mrs. Crawford, "that the Owenses were going to Bluewater for a rest. And then you sent me to Bluewater after them. And I got acquainted with Miss Owens and got her worked up and telling me—"

"Sure, Mamie, you're a good girl." Carroll cut her short.

"What about me?" growled the man who had trailed the Owens party. "You can give me a little credit, too!"

"Introducing Joe," Carroll said with a derogatory little laugh. "Joe, who failed to get the papers last night! Mercer, Joe is the head of our corps of investigators—or in plain talk, Joe and his boys hit the road and track down people or facts we're after. They pass themselves off as travelers, salesmen, or in a pinch, as private detectives."

"For instance?" said Mercer.

"For instance," said Joe. "I hung around Owens's hotel in St. Louis to see that that nurse didn't pull any fast ones and spirit him away. If she had—! It'd 've been unhealthy for her to try it."

"That nurse!" said Mrs. Crawford. "She's a nuisance."

"Yeah?" said Joe. "You're telling me? For instance, I went to her home town—Hilton it was—"

"That's right, Mr. Mercer," said Mrs. Crawford with satisfaction. "I worked it in Bluewater by advance appointment only—sounds exclusive, huh? That way I got the clients' names in advance, and it gave Joe here time to go dig up some facts I could startle them with. It was just a piece of luck that the nurse came with her mother, for a reading, the same day the Owens woman showed up. And was that young snip of a nurse impressed with me! I told some junk about her own family."

"Thanks to me, thanks to me," said Joe. "All the week before, I hung around this little burg of Hilton trying to find something on Ames." Here Cherry began to feel sick. "First, Mr. Mercer, I go to the Vital Records Building and find out Mrs. Ames's maiden name and her mother's name and who's dead in the family and when they died. That's good for the ghost act Mamie puts on. Then I sort of hang around town and keep my ears open. This Mr. Ames is in the real-estate game. So I go hang around the real-estate offices. Pretending I'm an out-of-town buyer, see? That way this Ames fellow tells me he's thinking of selling his own house. Then

Mamie has a ghost tell this stuff at the séance. It scares Kitty Owens so bad she loses her head and—"

"—so bad that," said Mrs. Crawford gleefully, "when I started mentioning Uncle Matthew, feeling her out, you know, to find out if we were on the right track on that old scandal, she screamed like a fool. That scream told me Uncle Matthew was the root of the trouble, all right."

"I also do a little strong-arm stuff, Mr. Mercer," Joe boasted. "For instance, last night—if anybody'd stopped me, I would've—" Cherry shuddered.

"Oh, we have it well organized," Gregory Carroll said.

Mercer said impatiently, "Let's get on. You've only explained how it works from the top, from you. Where do those four hundred fortunetellers all over the country come in? How much do they get of the take?" His voice was greedy and anxious.

"They get a pittance. Don't worry, Mercer. You and Thatch and I aren't risking the penitentiary for nickels and dimes. The big money stays right here." Cherry heard a sound which must have been Carroll slapping his pocket. She would have liked to see his saintly face at that moment. "Thatch, tell the new member of the firm how the small-time fortunetellers help us out."

"Certainly, with pleasure," came Mr. Thatch's voice. "They have only one job—to pry information out of the suckers and pass that information along to us. I keep a master file of information on all wealthy or prominent or influential people. Mr. Carroll and I keep everything we hear or dig up, as well as newspaper clippings. Then we pass some of that information along to the out-of-town fortunetellers, so they'll know which sucker is important enough to concentrate on, and what to say to him to force more information out of him."

Mercer objected, "Isn't it risky sending confidential blackmail stuff like that through the mails? There are postal regulations against it."

"Oh, we wouldn't do anything *illegal*," Mr. Thatch replied with a little laugh. "We avoid that risk in two ways, Mr. Mercer. First, we mail out what appears to be an innocent gossip column—it is a mimeographed bulletin, even has the suckers' photographs and license numbers of their cars. That advises the out-of-town fortunetellers in advance, so they can recognize the right suckers."

"But suppose a client walks in without appointment, without warning, and the fortuneteller never saw or heard of him before?"

"Often a client's license plates on his car are enough to identify him to these experts. Or they simply ask a few adroit questions. Then," said Mr. Thatch, "the out-of-town fortuneteller asks the client to wait, and quietly calls me up long-distance. He tells me over the phone whatever he could find out by himself, and I tell him whatever I have in the master file—within limits, of course. Then the local reader has, so to speak, a knife to put in the sucker's back. That is the way he can force out still more confidential information—the kind of information Mr. Carroll and I will eventually frame him with."

"I see, I see," said Mercer. "By long-distance telephone. Very clever."

Very clever, Cherry was thinking, and remembering the unexpected ring of a phone somewhere. Where was that? Where had that happened? She closed her eyes tightly and memory took her back to the overgrown rut in the road on the way to the witch's house. Wasn't it there she had thought she heard a telephone ring? Yes, it was, and she had dismissed the sound as imagination when she had seen the tumble-down shack. But there *had* been a phone in there! The witch had phoned Mr. Thatch! But how had she known Owens was coming?—they had had no appointment. Then Cherry remembered, too, the ten-minute wait while the witch did something in the other room. "Sick husband," she had said. Sick husband, indeed! That hag had been whispering into the telephone, and listening to Mr. Thatch.

"Yes, by telephone and by bulletin," Gregory Carroll repeated. "Also, one fortuneteller in the ring recommends a client to other fortunetellers in the ring. Some people are so crazy for fortunetellers, they go from one to another, like Kitty Owens. So we try to keep our suckers right in the family."

MISS AMES IS "DETAINED" 193

"I sent Kitty Owens to The Witch," Mrs. Crawford remarked. "Told her I was doing her a great favor, and she couldn't get there fast enough!"

Cherry behind the sofa sighed for Miss Kitty's folly.

"And I advised her to consult Lucy Pride," Mr. Thatch said. "I am not certain it was worth the trouble. I played the helpful errand boy and bought all Miss Owens's railroad tickets for their tour, so I could discover their itinerary. Once I learned what towns they would be in, I notified our fortunetellers in those towns and urged Miss Owens to go to see them."

"Pride isn't worth a nickel cigar to us," Joe said disgustedly. "We'll have to get rid of her, before she squeals on us."

"She won't squeal on us," Carroll said dryly. "Remember she's honestly psychic and remember she got into trouble with the police in her town for telling fortunes. She didn't know how to get around the law like we do. We showed her how. Remember she was absolutely alone, too. Why, she was a starving seamstress when we paid her bail and trapped her into working with us. We'll let her starve again and face the police again if she doesn't—ah—cooperate."

So little Miss Pride was as much a victim of Carroll as the clients! Cherry's heart turned over in pity, particularly at Mr. Thatch's next words:

"Mr. Mercer, Lucy Pride is a character! We pay her *only half* of what we pay anyone else and she does not even suspect it! Or if she did, she would be too frightened to say so."

"I wish The Witch were as easy to handle," Carroll remarked. "That tough old faker—there's nothing she wouldn't do for money. She boldly threatened to expose us to the police. She's corrupt all the way through, a born racketeer," he said in admiration. "But we have something on her and we keep her poor enough so she'll have to go on working for us."

"All right, all right," said Mercer, impatient again. "So much for the details. I still don't understand why I've had to duck around calling myself Fuller or James Smith, or why I had to let you use my Merriam Avenue house. I've certainly been taking a lot on faith."

"We've had to move around on account of that blamed nurse of Owens's," said Gregory Carroll. "I tried to scare her off—warned her not to meddle—I knew when I first saw her that she was aggressive. I knew she'd come looking for us."

Cherry grinned to herself.

"How'd you have liked to talk over our plans to squeeze Owens, some place where that nurse might be listening?" Carroll demanded. "That's why we had to move around—to get out of earshot."

Cherry clapped her hand over her mouth lest she laugh out loud. But this was no time to laugh—trapped in here. She listened soberly. She was almost sure now that she was going to hear something of use to Scott Owens.

"And the red wig?" Mercer asked derisively.

Carroll laughed. Joe said gruffly, "I told him not to do it. I told him red was too noticeable. I told him he didn't need no wig at all."

"Yes, I did need some disguise," said Carroll. "I'm pretty well known. My eyes give me away. I had to choose a wig more striking than my eyes."

Mr. Thatch tittered. "Why, you've always had a fancy to wear a red wig! This time you had an excuse. Gregory, you are a born actor!"

"All right, all right, the red wig was a stunt," Mercer cut in. "But it still seems to me I'm the only one who did anything useful. Sitting down there in the bank vault sorting papers until this nurse came in, and then following her back to Owens's house."

Cherry gasped. So she had been watched for what she took out of the safety deposit box, and where she went with the blue envelope! She was so excited she seemed to suffocate.

Joe said, "I thought you said neither The Witch or Pride could worm out of them where that box was? Of course, I've just come in off the road, I'm not up to date on the Owens case."

In a voice thick with gloating, Mamie Crawford said, "Kitty Owens told me that herself! Last week I just 'happened' to be in Des Moines when she was. She was all wrought up and when she 'heard' a good fortuneteller like me was in town, she came running to me as fast as her legs would carry her. For advice. She confided all her troubles to me—how the wicked, wicked Mr. Carroll was going to blackmail her poor, dear brother, and how papers proving her brother's innocence were lying in their box at the Fourth City Bank right here in this city, and the nurse was going to get them."

"So then," said Mercer, and his voice sounded amused, "I rented a safety deposit box, too, at the Fourth City Bank and—"

"Exactly," said Carroll impatiently. "But what's our next move to be?"

Cherry could see him pacing up and down the room in thought. He came so near her she could have touched his trouser cuff. At this point, Cherry had an overwhelming impulse to sneeze. She clamped one finger over her upper lip and held back the sneeze. Oh, why had Miss Kitty talked—why hadn't she—

"Just a minute," Mercer said. "How much does Bixby know?"

"Bixby? The superintendent here? He knows nothing. I gave him a good, fat tip to 'preserve our privacy,' as the management calls it. Bixby has merely been doing his job."

"Another thing I'd like to know," Mercer said. "I still haven't got head nor tail of this Owens story."

"I can give you a complete report on it," Mr. Thatch said.

Cherry trembled all over. Every word he spoke burned into her brain.

Twenty years ago Scott Owens was a young man, barely out of his teens. He was as hypersensitive, as impractical, as ignorant of money matters, then as now. He and his sister Kitty were alone, poor, and struggling to get Scott started on his musical career. Their name then was not Owens but Austin. Their only relative was an uncle, Matthew Austin, a driving, well-to-do businessman who had no use for artists "and such tomfoolishness."

Occasionally and grudgingly, Matthew Austin gave the young brother and sister a little money to tide them over. He had often said to them, and had written to Kitty in letters, that while he heartily disapproved of Scott's becoming a musician instead of a businessman, he would not let them starve.

"Then came an emergency," said Mr. Thatch with satisfaction. "The budding pianist and his sister were down to their last few dollars. Scott had a chance, under particularly good auspices, to give his first recital, if only he could pay two hundred dollars toward the rental of a concert hall. It all had to be done in a hurry. Uncle Matthew had been promising them some funds."

Mr. Thatch chuckled. "That promise was enough for excitable, impractical Scott. Without consulting the uncle or Kitty, he hastily wrote out a check and signed the uncle's name to it. He thought that since it was family funds, already promised to him, and the same family name, that he had every right to do so. He then went ahead and gave the recital which was a great success.

"But Uncle Matthew was offended to the core," Mr. Thatch gleefully went on. "Whether such a flighty, ignorant way of doing things offended his businessman's sense of orderliness, or whether it nettled him to see Scott come off a musical success when he had always predicted failure, is hard to know. At any rate, Uncle Matthew asked a punishment far in excess of Scott's blunder. He brought Scott to court on a charge of forgery, and had the artist—then about as old as that nurse of his—put in jail for two years."

Cherry's heart turned over. She waited tensely while Mr. Thatch ruffled through some papers. Then he went on:

"Kitty did all she could to free her brother. Only Uncle Matthew could help, by withdrawing his charge. Matthew refused to do that."

"But Scott was no forger, no criminal," Mercer interrupted, "only an impractical, unbusinesslike boy. Took his uncle's promise of funds a little too literally."

"But the law reads that Scott had committed forgery," Mr. Thatch responded dryly. "He had to spend, and did spend, two years in prison."

He continued with his report: Scott had emerged shamed, publicly disgraced, his health broken. Under Kitty's courageous guidance, they took the name of

MISS AMES IS "DETAINED" 199

Owens, their mother's name, and moved to the other end of the country. Scott started his musical career all over again.

Uncle Matthew had died some years later, thoroughly ashamed of what he had done to an innocent boy. He had written Scott letters to this effect, absolving him of all blame—letters which Scott had never answered. But Kitty had kept the letters, and had kept the earlier ones from Uncle Matthew offering the funds which Scott accepted by the wrong method. These letters were the proof of Scott's innocence, and they lay in the blue envelope which Joe had tried to steal.

"And you planned to—?" Mercer started to ask. The phone rang. Cherry nearly suffocated with anxiety while Carroll talked on the phone, and then Mr. Thatch resumed his report.

The blackmailers planned to drag out this old scandal via old newspaper accounts and old photographs of Scott. Ignoring Scott's innocence, they would notify the world that the celebrated pianist was nothing but a forger and a jailbird. Scott's only defense, and a weak one, was the letters from Uncle Matthew. Unless Scott paid off, the blackmailers were ready to ruin him utterly.

Again Cherry saw Carroll pacing up and down, thinking. He agitatedly swung his keys on a key ring around and around on his finger. His feet moved near Cherry. The keys dropped to the floor with a little clatter. Carroll bent to retrieve them. But he did not straighten up, for his eyes looked directly into Cherry's.

"Well, look who's here," he said dryly. Cherry gasped. His luminous eyes were like blue ice. "Come on. Get up out of there."

Cherry rose shakily to her feet. Carroll motioned to her to go stand in the middle of the room. All eyes were trained on her, like guns.

"How much have you heard?" Carroll demanded to know.

Mr. Thatch gave her a hostile glance. "She must have been here since before we came in. She's heard everything. Haven't you? Haven't you!"

"Y-yes." Cherry's mind stopped, paralyzed with fear. What were they going to do with her? She could think of nothing to do, to say, in her helplessness. It was all she could manage to continue standing upright. These five cold unscrupulous people were capable of anything.

Joe said it. "Rub her out."

"No," said Carroll. He rubbed his upper lip, thinking. Mamie Crawford tossed her tarnished yellow head at Cherry, sniffed, and looked disdainfully away. Mercer smoked in silence.

"We can't let her go," Carroll said at length. "We'll have to detain Miss Ames." He said her name sarcastically, very formally, like an insult. "Detaining Miss Ames may prove to be of help." He added threats, clear and terrible.

MISS AMES IS "DETAINED"

Cherry was terrified. She knew too much. Her mind began to move again, faster now, and in earnest. "Detained" by a gang of cutthroats like these! But why? What did they want of her? They couldn't afford to let her go—they knew she would inform the police. But aside from that, how would detaining her do them any good? *What else* did they want of her? In a burst of shrewd inspiration, she thought, "Appeal to their self-interest! Pretend to be on their side!"

Aloud she said, "I'm not so crazy about Owens as you think."

This was received in disbelieving silence. Joe cleaned his fingernails. Carroll demanded, "Then why are you trying to help Owens?"

Cherry said stolidly, "He sent me. It's my job. I'm stuck with him."

"A likely story. Why don't you leave the case?"

"And starve? He pays well." She added softly, "He pays *very* well, Mr. Carroll."

Carroll smiled grimly. "I see what you mean."

Cherry waited. She was afraid she might say the wrong thing and spoil the little credence she had gained. Better to keep silent, let Carroll take the lead; she would follow his hints.

He asked suddenly, "You went to Owens's safety deposit box. You have the key and, I suppose, a power of attorney. Have you still got them?"

"Yes. They're in Owens's house."

Carroll thought again. Mamie Crawford said, "Don't trust her."

Carroll looked up at Mr. Thatch. "We need—proof. We've got to *back up* our charges—otherwise there's no provable blackmail angle, only slander, unless we can get—"

"The change of name papers?" Cherry put in quickly. Her mind was racing. "They're still in the vault." It was a long shot, Cherry realized, but it might help to get her out of here. She had to do something!

Carroll swung around and glared at her. Then slowly relaxing against his chair, he addressed Thatch.

"We need those papers, Thatch, before we can act. If anything," he mused, "they're even more valuable to us than the letters. With those in my hand, I could pounce."

"Then send this nurse for them," Thatch suggested, "I know you don't trust her but she knows everything, anyway. And I really must tell you again," Mr. Thatch reasoned, "that I cannot locate the change of name papers by legal search. I don't know the year Scott Owens changed his name nor in what state he did it. It would take me five years to trace it—when the change of name papers are undoubtedly right there in the vault—and this nurse has the key! Use your head, Gregory. We must not wait on this—Owens might die in the meantime and then where would we be?"

MISS AMES IS "DETAINED"

Carroll turned to Cherry, who was sick at their callousness. "Listen, Ames. I don't trust you but I don't have to. Because you'll end up in the river if you play us dirty. Understand?" Cherry solemnly nodded. "But if you play it smart," Carroll said more pleasantly, "there's a nice chunk of cash in it for you."

Cherry's hopes leaped. They were going to afford her a means of escape! She might save herself and Scott yet!

"If—if you want proof," Cherry said breathlessly, "I can tell you that—that the letters are in the wall safe at home—in a blue envelope—and that Owens's deposit box is stuffed with papers. There's a jewel box in there, too." *Just let them try and get it,* she thought fiercely. *Those things are safe. They could guess what's in that box, anyway. Anything to make them believe I'm working with them.*

"A jewel box?" Mercer was interested. "She talks sense."

"All right." Carroll had made his decision. "Now listen carefully, Ames. We're holding you here until ten-thirty tonight. Oh, yes, Ames," he hissed softly when he noticed her jump in alarm. "Until ten-thirty tonight. We'll 'escort' you home then. Tomorrow morning at nine-thirty you be at the vault, understand? Get the change of name papers. Never mind the jewelry. Get the change of name papers. And don't forget to bring the letters from the wall safe. Come directly here with them."

Cherry protested that her patient was ill, had had an attack that morning, and needed her right away.

"I thought that all out, Ames. You step to the phone there and give instructions to the housekeeper. Tell her you've been unavoidably detained, but will be there about eleven tonight. And remember, Ames, no funny stuff."

Cherry had no choice in the matter but to follow out Carroll's directions.

At ten-thirty that night, Carroll gave Cherry a final warning before she was released. "Remember, be at the vault at nine-thirty A.M., Ames, and come directly here with the papers and the letters. And remember, also, we're tapping Owens's telephone wires. Don't try any funny business. Joe here will be following you from this minute on. And just one more word of caution," he added menacingly, "don't let either the housekeeper or her husband step out of the house or they'll get hurt. I don't care how you manage that—that's your problem—but remember, it will be healthier for them to stay indoors tonight and tomorrow morning."

Cherry gulped and nodded her head in agreement.

Then Carroll opened the door and let her out. Joe followed her.

It was ludicrous to think that only a short time ago she had had hopes. Now she was completely trapped. Joe's footsteps sounded behind her.

CHAPTER XIII

Trapped!

TO KNOW EVERY DETAIL OF THE BLACKMAILERS' schemes—and to be unable to lift a finger against them—To be forced, not merely to stand helplessly by, but to *help* them strike at Scott Owens— This to Cherry was the final, bitter irony. So this was what efforts to help Scott had led to!

She suffered an unspeakable wretchedness. The echoes of the man's footsteps sounded behind her constantly, in her imagination and in fact.

Several times, during that terrible night, Cherry lifted the receiver from the telephone, only to put it despairingly down again. Twice in the night shadows, she tried slipping out of the house, but two husky men, whom she had never seen before, patrolled the sidewalk in front of the Owens house, and Joe himself lay hidden in the back garden. Cherry was caught tight—she could do nothing. Finally in despair she threw herself on the bed.

Wild plans of escape shaped up out of the shadows. Set the house afire! Get out in the confusion and report Carroll! But the excitement could kill Mr. Scott—and one did not actually, deliberately set a house on fire. Try telephoning anyway! No, that was hopeless: the wires were tapped and no mistake. Go to a telegraph office and send a telegram to the police? "Yes," Cherry thought ironically, "with that gangster looking over my shoulder as I write the telegram!"

Toward daylight she fell into a fitful sleep. Her nightmares anguished her so, that she rose and bathed and dressed, more tired than when she had gone to bed, and then waited for the household to awaken. It was an eternity of loneliness and foreboding.

At eight Mr. Scott woke up. "I don't feel so well today, Cherry," he said. "Must I really eat breakfast?"

"You must eat something," Cherry said, and sat with him and coaxed the food down. It took every ounce of Cherry's will power to concentrate on feeding him for she was consciously aware of the clock relentlessly ticking away the precious minutes.

It was nine o'clock! Cherry hurried in search of Jen and Lucien and found them in the kitchen, enjoying a peaceful snack. Cherry shuddered at a mental picture of these two nice souls being tortured by the gangsters.

Quickly, giving them no time to ask questions, she demanded that they both stay within Mr. Scott's call—both of them—Mr. Scott was ill and under no condition were either of them to leave the house until she got back—she had an important errand to do for Mr. Scott and would be back just as fast as she possibly could—her words came tumbling out. Before they had the chance to say anything, she ran quickly out of the kitchen and dashed up the stairs to her room.

Nine-fifteen! Cherry couldn't repress the shudder that shook her.

She slapped on her hat, grabbed up her purse, gloves, the vault key, and Miss Owens's letter giving her power of attorney. She opened the front door and froze to the top step, looking around for the man. There Joe was, across the street, watching for her. She walked down the street, and heard him behind her. Numbly she got on a streetcar. He got on too, and sat across the aisle from her. His face, which she saw fully for the first time, was coarse and brutal. He never took his eyes from Cherry.

Nine-thirty o'clock!

Cherry got off the streetcar, pushed into the bank's revolving doors, and caught a reflected glimpse of the man in the glass of the doors.

She walked across the marble bank corridor, her heels tapping, the heavy, ruthless footsteps dogging her. Busy men and women filled the bank. Cherry longed to cry out to them for help. She walked steadily, mechanically on, as in a bad dream—only this was no dream, this was real.

Down the stairs she went and along the airless basement corridor. The man came right behind her, like evil itself pursuing her, into this subterranean place of bright electric lights.

At the barred door to the first, office room, the guard glanced at the key in Cherry's hand and unlocked the iron door. "Good morning," the guard said pleasantly. Cherry swallowed hard and walked through. Joe quickly slipped in with her. The guard locked the door again.

"We're together," Joe said to the guard. He took a cruel grip on Cherry's arm. "I'm staying right with you," he said under his breath. "I'm not giving you any chance to try anything, see?"

Cherry felt so choked with fear and grief that she could hardly breathe. With the loathesome man at her side, she went through the routine of showing an office manager her power of attorney, showing the key to the box, signing a verified signature for access to Owens's box, and, finally, she received the stamped slip of paper. Her mind was no longer functioning in orderly fashion: questions like "What will Scott think when he checks back and finds *my* signature?"—broken bit of pictures of Scott in court, Scott at home stricken with a heart attack, Carroll's cold smile and Mercer's greedy face—

"Get a move on," Joe muttered, and roughly but imperceptibly shoved her toward the inner vault room. "The change of name papers. Go on, get them!"

Cherry stepped through the huge circular steel doorway, where the room-sized safe stood open, her slip of paper and the key in her hand. Joe started to step through with her when one of the armed guards in the inner vault room barred his way.

"Your key and slip, sir?"

"I'm goin' in with my wife. She has 'em."

"Sorry, sir, only the person with the key and slip can go in."

Joe glared at Cherry over the guard's shoulder.

"Well, hurry up about it, then!"

The guard said, "I can give you the box, ma'am, and you can take it outside, and you and your husband can go into one of the little private rooms."

Outside? No! What little safety she might have lay here, in this barred, guarded, armed room with its—

"We'll keep the box in here," Cherry hastily answered the guard. Joe looked as if he wanted to kill her.

... this inner vault room with its armed bank guards, its emergency barred door (Cherry's mind raced on), its emergency telephone— And Joe in the first office room with *its* locked barred entrance door, and *its* full complement of armed guards. She nearly wept for joy as the chance—for safety!—burst full blown on her in this perilous instant. *Joe was locked in! Joe was surrounded by armed men and outnumbered*! And she could throw an emergency gate between herself and this killer! And she could use that emergency telephone to reach the police!

"Close this vault door!" she yelled. "And don't let that man get away!" She pointed at Joe. With the other hand she tugged at the barred emergency gate and slammed it shut between herself and him.

"Don't let him go! Thief! Stop thief!"

Joe reached inside his jacket for his gun and ran for the locked outer door. Instantly four guards in the office room were on him, their own guns out of their holsters. Joe ran again, dodging them, to the vault door. A shot boomed out, echoing thunderously in these underground vaults. Cherry shiveringly thought it must be Joe's gun, aimed at her. The four guards locked inside the vault room with her pulled her into a corner, out of Joe's range. Their own guns drawn and aimed at Joe, they edged around but not directly before the barred emergency door. One of them kept Cherry covered while she begged to use the telephone in here. It was on a metal folding extension, at the now-closed emergency gate, and swung safely out of range of Joe's gun. Joe was shouting. He ran again as guards tried to corner him. The office workers and two box holders cowered behind desks. The guards outside scuffled with him—a desk was flung over with a crash—but Cherry was intent only

TRAPPED! 211

on the telephone. Emergency alarm bells were ringing.

"Police! Police! Hurry!" she signaled the operator. "Hello! Please go immediately to the apartment of Gregory Carroll at"— she gave the address and the names of the four people waiting for her to bring the papers— "the charge? The charge is, they're threatening Scott Owens with extortion! Yes, the famous pianist!"

"We'll take him into protective custody," came the deep voice over the wire.

Cherry remembered to say, "He's sick, don't move him!"

By the time she hung up, the outer office room of this place teemed with blue-coated policemen. Cherry saw them handcuff Joe and drag him off. He shouted curses at her, threats, vile words. Cherry shook all over. She still held fast to the key. The box was still unopened, still in its place in the shining steel wall. The change of name papers were safe.

A bank guard opened the emergency door and two policemen strode into the vault to Cherry.

In a daze Cherry obediently answered their questions and followed them to the street. They climbed into a police wagon where Joe already sat, manacled to his captors. Cherry looked away.

The hours at the police station were like a dreary nightmare—hours in which Cherry answered the same questions over and over again—hours in which Carroll,

Mr. Thatch, Mercer, and Mrs. Crawford were brought in, a sullen, cowed group, furiously denying everything, refusing to admit even that they recognized Cherry.

But the police had raided the headquarters apartment, ransacked it, had found there and taken dozens of confidential files, so-called "gossip bulletins," telegrams, lists of auto license plates, damning evidence of all kinds.

When Cherry was finally permitted to leave, and the station door was opened onto the street for her, she was surprised to find that it was night, and dark. She was so tired, so dazed. She began to walk automatically, back to the Owens house.

She found the house blazing with lights and excitement, and policemen at the door. She had expected that. She was questioned before being admitted to the house.

But what Cherry had not expected to see was Scott Owens downstairs, fully dressed, beaming, obviously in better health than he had possessed in weeks—since Carroll had made his threat.

The musician came toward her, with that smile that welled up from deep in his gentle eyes.

"Cherry—Cherry, my dear—" He took her hand. "There's no way to tell you how I—how much I— Oh, Cherry, my brave little nurse!"

CHAPTER XIV

Troubles and Triumphs

A PARTY WAS IN FULL SWING IN THE DOWNSTAIRS LIVing rooms. Bébé with great gusto was playing Scott's new waltz. The beautiful, dark Carmela stood beside Bébé at the first piano and sang it, gaily making up words as she went along. Dr. Pratt was here too this Sunday afternoon, giving out broad smiles and clouds of cigar smoke, as he talked to Miss Kitty. The pianist's sister was a considerably chastened lady, since she had returned and learned all that had happened. But Scott himself was beaming and pouring out punch for the white-haired orchestra conductor, Dr. White, and Mrs. White. Jen beamed too, at Scott, and even the abstracted Lucien, stepping over the three poodles, with an armful of music scores, and Octave the cat on his shoulder, seemed happier though without knowing quite why. Perhaps the happiest person present was Cherry.

For this party—though the guests did not know it—was a celebration of the end of Scott Owens's troubles. Carroll and his ring were under prosecution and would never again harm the musician. The police had kept Scott's confidential papers confidential; they did not and would not expose his unhappy past. Scott was safe now. The entire affair was closed, for good.

Miss Kitty, sitting here on the divan large and capable-looking in her green dress, still wore a dazed expression. Scott had not minced words with her when she had returned home two days ago.

"This mess was your doing, Kit," he had said bluntly, in Cherry's presence. "If it hadn't been for your weak-headed superstition, and your wagging tongue, this ugly business need never have happened."

Miss Kitty had hung her reddish head. "It's true, Scott. I'm sorry. I'm ashamed. For me, such a *practical* person, to—" Then she had brightened. "But you did get out of it all right."

"Despite you! And because of little Cherry here. Kit, Kit, you still don't see the enormity of your folly! I don't suppose you ever will."

Cherry had smiled and suggested mischievously, "Maybe you ought to try being a little less practical, Miss Kitty."

The police had told the Owenses and Cherry a little of the background of the people who had been tormenting them. Gregory Carroll had a long criminal record. Starting as a poor boy, dishonest, cold, shallowly clever, he had always believed "only fools work." He had never worked honestly for a living, but relied instead on get-rich-quick rackets. Caught and sent to jail over and over again, he therefore claimed "the whole world was against him" and so "had more reason than ever" to cheat people and seize for himself. He had changed his name and identity several times, but not for a decent reason like Scott's.

Mr. Thatch was quite another story. He had come of a well-to-do family and had been educated in several universities, here and abroad. For many years he had been a professor, living alone. He had led a humdrum, solitary, and narrow life. In middle age he had done a surprising thing. He had started taking drugs. These were expensive, illegal, and necessitated much money. Mr. Thatch stole, very cleverly, over a period of years from his own school. When he was finally discovered, his teaching career was forever closed to him and he was sent to prison. There he met Gregory Carroll, on one of his more recent charges. Carroll at once recognized how useful Mr. Thatch's trained mind could be to his own warped ends. The totally demoralized Mr. Thatch accepted Carroll's offer because it meant enough money to buy more drugs.

Joe's story was no less sordid. He had at one time worked at menial but honest jobs for his living. But it paid him better to be strong-arm man for Carroll. In his stupid, limited way, he resented his cleverer boss and was jealous of his rich mode of living. Joe had informed on Carroll to the police in a way that would tack on an extra ten years to Carroll's sentence.

Mercer was simply a shady business man who, at last, stepped on the wrong side of the law. Mrs. Crawford was a widow, a sorry shabby woman buffeted around by hard luck and no principles. She had never been a match for Carroll.

Cherry did not want to think about these ugly people. She had defeated them and so had earned the right, now, to dismiss them from her mind.

Cherry's work here was finished. Mr. Scott was very much better. He did not need her any more. "And almost best of all," her face dimpled, "Dr. Pratt lavishly praised my nursing. I guess I feel pretty good about my work here. Yes, relieved, and very, very good."

Cherry's good-byes were quickly made, to the accompaniment of a houseful of music. Miss Kitty thanked her with sincere emotion. Dr. Pratt thumped her approvingly on the shoulder. Only her good-bye to Mr. Scott was difficult.

He tilted up her chin with one finger and smiled down at her.

"Now see here, Miss Cherry Ames, I have one final order for you! As long as I give recitals, I shall send you tickets and expect to see you sitting there in the front row!"

"It's—it's a date," Cherry smiled back shakily, and fled before the sentimental tears spilled over. Music rang out behind her as her taxi pulled away for the railroad station. Scott Owens's music would ring in her memory for years to come.

Hilton, when she arrived in the early summer evening, looked quiet, plain, substantial, and very dear. The little town was having its Sunday evening supper, except for the Ames family who were waiting for Cherry. The two Fortunes were there waiting for Cherry, too.

They all sat down together at the big table under a circle of light. Cherry was in her usual chair between her father and Charlie. Midge and Dr. Joe smiled at her across the table.

"Being home feels good," Cherry said delightedly. "No more private duty nursing for me!"

"Why, Cherry!" her mother said. "The nurses' registry called up only yesterday asking for you to take a case!"

Dr. Joe nodded his gray head. "I told them you were coming home and they're eager to have you."

Cherry grinned. "Well, I'll call 'em right back and tell 'em to take my name off their list. Permanently."

Charlie grinned back at her. "What are you up to next, scamp? Come on, confess, we know you!"

Cherry shook back her black curls. "Oh—ah—I'm not saying—may I have some iced tea, please?"

Midge groaned. "Cherry, you can't give up private duty nursing. Not now! You positively can't!"

"Why not, for goodness' sake?"

"Because I—" The teen-ager wailed and all eyes turned on her. She pulled back a lock of hair and, rather proudly, displayed a red rash on her cheek. "I think I have—don't scold me, Dad—the measles!"

"Midge!" Dr. Fortune was horrified. "Why didn't you tell me?"

"Because I want Cherry to nurse me and I was waiting for her to come home!"

Cherry shut her eyes, took a deep breath in chagrin, and then burst out laughing.

"All right, all right, Midge, I'll nurse you and your measles! But you are absolutely my last private duty case. Because I have a mighty important date with the Spencer Club! In fact, I guess I have a date with a brand-new nursing career!"